PHILLIP & WHIZZY
TRILOGY

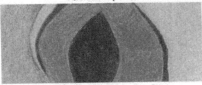

LAND OF MISTASIA

RETURN TO MISTASIA

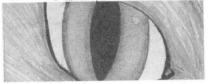

LAST EMERALD

Available

in

Paperback and Kindle™

www.Amazon.com/Kindle

Keyword: Mistasia

1

RETURN TO MISTASIA

PHILLIP & WHIZZY TRILOGY (BOOK 2)

Written & Illustrated by

Christopher M. Purrett

www.LandOfMistasia.com

www.ChristopherMPurrett.com

To my daughters Lea and Kyra, may this
remind you that every day brings a
different adventure. For my wife, Misty,
your continued love inspires me every day.

Library of Congress
Purrett, Christopher M.
Phillip & Whizzy: Return To Mistasia / by Christopher M. Purrett
p. cm.

Summary: Phillip and Whizzy return to Mistasia to battle sorcerer
LaCroiux who is attempting to free his leader, Cragon Cadieux.
ISBN 97809833278-2-0
[1. Fantasy – Fiction. 2. Science Fiction – Fiction. 3. Wizards –
Fiction. 4. Heroes – Fiction.]

Released in United States of America
First Edition, August 2011

CHAPTERS

LAND OF MISTASIA

KEEGAN CASTLE

DEADLY SPRAY FOREST

MAMMOTH GORGE

ADAIR VILLAGE

MICHI MOUNTAINS

RED RIVER

CADIEUX CASTLE

WOLVERINE FOREST

DRAGON LAKE

CADIEUX VILLAGE

WHIZZENMOG HOME

TERASOAR ISLAND

UNKNOWN LANDS

COLOSSAL LANDS

MICHAEL WHIZZENMOG

1

My name is Michael Whizzenmog the Third, but my friends call me "Whizzy". I live in a small quiet town called Greenville, but last summer I found out that I am a wizard, and my twin sister is a witch. Apparently, our family is really from another world...or place, well whatever it is, called Mistasia.

My best friend, Phillip Harper, and I traveled to Mistasia to save my sister from an evil king, Cragon Cadieux, who was a sorcerer that had ruled Mistasia for nearly a decade.

Phillip was normally a scared, awkwardly tall boy, but in Mistasia he was a green frog with superpowers. Weird, huh?

Anyway, we traveled to Mistasia through a portal in my basement, saved my sister, defeated the evil sorcerer and helped Princess Merran, Cragon's niece, become queen. That's the very short version.

After summer ended we had to go back to school, and now I'm a freshman at Greenville High School. The first couple of weeks were awful. New school! New teachers and new bullies! I hated being a freshman.

My sister Rachel stuck up for Phillip and me when she could...something she never would have done last year. I could tell she missed being a witch.

The first thing I got excited about all school year was Winter break! Just before it started I began having dreams about Mistasia. In the dream, I could see Grace Tallon, our elven guide and protector for Queen Merran. I wondered if we would ever be there again.

That day would come much sooner than I expected.

I DON'T WANNA GO TO SCHOOL
2

"Ugh! What is that sound?" I rolled over in my bed and opened my stinging eyes. My head spun like I had just been on an amusement park ride for days. My alarm clock buzzed its annoying tone. It was a cross between a fire alarm and an injured cat...mostly because I beat it viciously every time it went off. Swinging my arm like a hammer, I smashed into the clock and knocked it onto the floor. "I don't wanna go to school." I said that every morning...like it would magically change my fortune. It never did. I always had to go to school.

After struggling out of bed and getting dressed, I dragged myself to the bathroom to brush my teeth.

I stared into the mirror. My fiery hair wildly waved back at me with every movement. I hadn't had a hair cut in about three months and so it sort of resembled octopus tentacles hanging off my head. Each eye blinked independently, and my eyelids felt so heavy.

"Toothbrush...Toothbrush? Where the heck is my...?" I searched through the drawers without luck. After slamming the drawer to my right in disgust, a voice startled me.

"Michael, sweetheart? You're up early." It was my mother.

Early? I thought. I got up for school at this time everyday.

My mom stood in the bathroom doorway with a stunned look on her face.

"I'm getting ready, Mom," I snapped.

"Michael Whizzenmog, you watch your tone young man!" She didn't sound happy.

I didn't even want to look her in the eye. She had a way of making me feel guilty about my attitude. The sensation of her glaring down at me burned the side of my neck. She waited patiently for an apology. I couldn't take it any longer.

I exhaled, "Sorry, Mom."

"Thank you, Michael."

She disappeared from the doorway and walked down the hallway.

I opened the drawer to my left and found my toothbrush. As I reached for it, I heard my mom call to me from down the hall.

"Yeah, Mom?" I called as I poked my head into the hallway to hear her better.

"Michael, you know it *is* Winter break. You don't have school today!"

My shoulders dropped and my toothbrush fell out of my mouth and onto the floor. I muttered inappropriate things under my breath so she wouldn't hear. I had forgotten to turn my alarm off and now I was awake...way too early.

Two hours later my twin sister, Rachel, came bouncing down the stairs, happy and perky as usual.

"Morning, Whizzy!"

I just groaned as I lay with my head resting on the arm of the couch.

"Well! Someone's happy this morning," she responded.

"Your brother forgot to turn his alarm off," my mom interjected from the kitchen.

Rachel just laughed and went in to join her.

I rolled toward the back of the couch and buried my face in the cushion. **Shut up!** I yelled into the couch.

"What's wrong, Michael?"

"Nothing, Mom!" I quickly responded as I bolted up into a seated position.

Why does she have to be so happy? I wondered about my sister. I might still challenge the fact that we were actually twins. We don't even look alike. She had long straight reddish-brown hair, green eyes and was about four inches taller than me. That's right...my twin sister was taller than me. It is awful. People at school think she is pretty...Pretty? I don't even want to go there.

It didn't matter. She had been really nice to me this school year. We almost never talked in middle school. Now, after what happened in Mistasia last summer, she was different.

"Michael. Breakfast is ready!"

Well, at least Phillip will be here this afternoon!

WAYS TO AVOID MY SISTER

3

After breakfast I paced around my house waiting for Phillip to arrive. I was bored out of my mind. Sitting still isn't one of my best traits. I would sit on the couch in the basement for a couple of minutes. Then, I would walk around the couch before sitting back down again.

When the doorbell rang, I dashed upstairs leaping three steps at a time, which is a lot for my short legs.

"I got it! I got it! I got it!" I yelled at my sister as we both reached for the door handle. "I got it," I said in a little bit calmer voice.

"Alright," Rachel replied while giving me a peculiar expression. I think she was questioning my sanity at that point.

Rachel stood next to me waiting. I didn't open the door though. I glanced at her, then the door before looking back at her again.

"What?" She snapped. "Open the door."

"Are you gonna stand there?" I asked.

"Whizzy, what's wrong with you?"

"What? Nothing's wrong with me. Don't you have to go do your hair or something?" I sounded like an idiot. Then, the doorbell rang again.

"I wanted to say 'hi' to Phillip," Rachel replied. She seemed hurt that I was questioning what she was doing, like she was Phillip's best friend.

"Well, he's here to see me!" I almost couldn't believe I said it. I was fighting with my sister over my best friend...who just happened to like my sister.

"Whizzy, can you open the door?" Phillip's muffled voice came through. "It's really cold out here."

Suddenly, I snapped out of my haze and opened the door.

Phillip was bundled up in a light green jacket that had "GHS" embroidered on the chest in large white letters with a gold trim. The letters stood for Greenville High School. His floppy brown hair was hanging out from underneath his winter hat, which matched his jacket. He was now over six-feet tall and really skinny. I only came up to his chest.

Phillip had adjusted to high school much better than I did. I wouldn't be caught dead in our school's jacket.

"It's freezing out there," Phillip chattered. He rubbed his cold hands together.

Phillip Harper had been my best friend for as long as I could remember. He had also pined for my sister nearly as long.

"Hey, Rachel," Phillip smiled.

He wouldn't have been able to speak around her last year, but Mistasia changed him...all of us really. Last year Rachel wouldn't have been standing at the cold front door when Phillip got here either.

After a couple of awkward moments of them looking at each other I pulled him toward the basement and told Rachel she could talk to him later.

I spent most of the day attempting to avoid my sister. Every time Phillip and I would start something she would check in on us. First, we played bowling but only finished three frames. She came downstairs with sodas and pretzels, and the next thing I knew, her and Phillip were sitting on the couch together. Then, when we started watching a movie, "The Captain's Loot", an awesome story about pirates, she joined us. She even flopped right down between us. At one point, I thought she and Phillip were holding hands. Then, we played basketball...or maybe I should say dodge ball because I spent more time avoiding getting drilled in the face with the ball than anything. Phillip kept blocking all my shots. In my attempt to get Rachel to leave us alone, I had asked Phillip if he would play basketball...which I never do for two reasons. One, he is really tall, and two, he's on the high school junior varsity basketball team. Whenever we play, he kills me. Sometimes I don't even score. So technically, Rachel ruined my game with Phillip without even playing. Finally, I dragged Phillip upstairs to the one place that I figured my sister would never go...my bedroom. She says it smells funny, which I like because it keeps her away. However, our alone time didn't last very long. It was dinnertime.

MISTASIAN MATH

4

During dinner, I had talked my mom into letting Phillip spend the night. She usually never minded. It had been a few months since he was on the basketball team now. Most weekends he had had a game or practice, but now he had more free time. I didn't quite understand why he had joined the team...I guess it was because he was tall. He thought it helped him fit in. Phillip had somehow figured out how to work his body in the past couple of months, too. If he had tried to play a sport of any kind last year, it would have meant total humiliation. He struggled to walk and chew gum before, and now he suddenly figured out how to run and dribble a basketball without falling down.

Don't get me wrong...it's great! I go to every game. I hate basketball really, but he's my best friend. It just hasn't been the same since we got back from Mistasia...I almost wish we hadn't gone. Phillip and Rachel both had changed...for the better, but I still felt the same- small, angry all the time and ...well, I don't know.

Anyway, Phillip and I sat up watching television. We had moved back to the basement. Rachel hadn't come downstairs in a while, so I had started to relax. Neither of us talked. It was like there was nothing to say. When we did talk, it was about stupid things, like a commercial about shoes or some new video game. Then, Rachel startled me.

"Whizzy!" was all she said, but it scared the heck out of me. I almost fell off the couch.

"Jezz, Rachel! Don't sneak up on me like that."

Phillip started to laugh. I shot him a nasty glare.

"What do you want?" I snapped. My heart pounded in my chest. It echoed all the way into my ears.

"Sorry, Whizzy. I was just thinking. How long has it been?" She just looked at me as if I had any idea what she was talking about.

I could feel my frustration growing. Sometimes the slightest thing would get me going...and Rachel was at the top of the list of frustrations.

"Rachel, I have no idea what you are even asking me?

"Since when, Rachel?" Phillip asked trying to avoid my meltdown.

She sat down between us on the couch and looked behind us. I turned around to see what she was looking at. It was nothing...just the staircase. I thought she was losing her mind. Then, she unfolded a piece of paper in her hand. It had writing all over it. Maps, numbers, and drawings...it looked like Mistasia.

"Wow, is that Mistasia?" Phillip seemed overly interested.

Rachel nodded and then smiled. She pushed her hair back from her face and tucked it behind her ears.

I caught Phillip staring at her. He saw my expression and quickly refocused on the drawing in her hands.

"I can't figure this out. I hoped maybe you guys could help me."

"Sure!" Phillip answered.

"Fine," I replied out of disgust. I could see that my sister was never going to leave us alone.

"I was trying to do the math, but it just doesn't seem possible." Rachel pointed to a jumble of numbers in the upper right corner of the map she had sketched. Just next to the title "Mistasia", was her attempt to figure out something.

I had no idea what it was. "What are you doing? This is a mess." I barked and slid back on the couch.

Rachel shook her head in frustration. "If you would let me explain, Whizzy, I would tell you. I am trying to figure out how long it's been since we were in Mistasia."

"Well, it was right when we got outta school last year," Phillip replied eagerly.

"June 17th," I elaborated.

"Yes, I know. And today is December 15th. That makes two hundred and ten days," Rachel said as she refigured the math on her paper.

"Alright problem solved. Goodbye!" I quickly responded.

Phillip, however, got pretty upset. Sometimes I forgot that he liked my sister...apparently more than he favors our friendship. He didn't even look at me when he barked, "Shut up, Whizzy!" He never yelled at me. I was shocked and kind of angry actually.

"Guys, stop it!" Rachel pleaded before she continued. "I know it's been two hundred and ten days here in Greenville, but I am trying to figure out how long it has been for the people in Mistasia."

"Oh, well, how do we figure that out?" Phillip asked while he studied her math problem on the paper still in her hands. "Grace said that every day in Mistasia was equal to an hour here."

"Right!" Rachel responded. "That's what I thought she said, but that's impossible."

I sat up as I tried to do the Mistasian math in my head.

"No, we had only been gone for like a little more than five hours when we returned home remember," Phillip empathically responded.

"He's right, Rachel," I agreed. "It had only been five hours when we came back. The math would work."

"So what's wrong with that?" Phillip asked Rachel who seemed hesitant to give her answer.

"That would mean it's been more than thirteen years."

MOUSE IN THE WHIZZENMOG HOUSE

5

"Thirteen years!" Phillip and I replied in unison.

I turned the television on mute and tossed the remote on the floor.

"Does that mean Grace and Princess Merran are thirteen years older?" Phillip asked in astonishment.

"*Queen* Merran," Rachel corrected. "She became queen just before we left."

"That's unbelievable. It hasn't even been a year here. How does that happen?" I questioned. It made my head hurt to think about it.

"How did our sliding glass door turn into a spinning black portal to another world? None of it seems possible, but unless all three of us are having the same crazy dream, it happened." Rachel refolded her paper and put it in her jean pocket.

"What was that?" Phillip asked as if he had heard a noise.

"I didn't hear anything, Phillip," I said while listening intently.

"I thought I heard a squeaky giggle."

Rachel began to laugh. Then, I started laughing. Phillip seemed confused at first. Then, he joined us with a snort which made all of us laugh even harder.

But we quickly stopped. Standing on the carpet next to the television was a small black mouse. It stood on its hind legs and stared at us. It even seemed to smile.

Rachel screamed. I placed my hand over her mouth. It was almost midnight and our mom was sleeping upstairs.

"You'll wake up mom!" I whispered in her ear.

"It's a friggin' mouse, Whizzy."

"Phillip, get the sticks!" I demanded.

The mouse's expression changed violently from a smile to fear. Its eyes bulged and it yelped when Phillip handed me a hockey stick. We both dashed after the fleet-footed mouse as it darted around the basement's carpeted floor.

"Don't kill it, Whizzy," Rachel yelled. "Phillip, stop!" She started to cry.

"Are you kidding me? What do you want us to do with it?" I barked.

"Please, don't kill me!" A squeaky small voice echoed through the room. We all looked down at the black mouse as it was cowering in the corner.

"Oh no," I muttered. "Not again!"

Rachel exploded off the couch and ran between us almost knocking me down. "Are you from Mistasia?" She asked in excited anticipation.

"Yes, Rachel Whizzenmog," the black mouse responded.

She picked up the frightened creature and held him up in the air.

The three of us stared at yet another talking creature in our basement. This was the third in the past six months counting the snake that stole my sister for the sorcerer that worked for King Cragon and Grace Tallon who appeared as an eagle.

"I am Aevion. I am a servant to the Queen. Commander Tallon sent me here to ask for your help." The scared mouse pleaded. He rubbed his paws in a jittery fashion.

"Grace!" I responded. My heart jumped at the thought of her. I wanted to see her, and had always hoped she would return some day. "What's wrong?"

"Commander Tallon needs your assistance. I do not know for what purpose. I am only a humble servant to the Queen. I am not an elven warrior. I only know that the commander was headed to The Deadly

Spray Forest after sending me through the portal."

"What is it with the forests in Mistasia?" I thought aloud. "Why can't there be a Happy Cheerful Forest?"

"Aevion, how can we help?" Rachel asked.

"Do you have your wands?" He asked.

WHIZZENMOG WANDS

6

I rummaged through my closet. It was a disaster. I had been tossing things in here all school year. My mom had been yelling at me to clean it up. Right about now, I wished I had listened to her.

I grabbed my backpack and slung it over my shoulder, nearly winging Phillip in the head. Actually, it was a pretty good toss considering he was over six-feet tall now.

"Watch out, Whizzy!"

"Sorry," I replied while continuing to pull things from my closet. I found all sorts of things. My English paper about Edgar Allan Poe...it was due over a month ago. I never thought to look in the closet. Then, I discovered a half-eaten sandwich from like October.

"That is disgusting!" Phillip said. I thought I heard him gag just a bit.

"I know; it reminds me of you last summer, Phillip." I held up the now green piece of bread.

"This is going to take forever, Whizzy. We need to go...now!" Phillip was so excited. I think he even started licking his lips like a frog after eating a fly.

"I know. I thought it was in here."

"Are you sure?" Phillip asked. "I mean could it be somewhere else? I'll go look if you just tell me where?"

"Ah, ha!" I interrupted as I pulled out a woody colored object.

"You found it!" Phillip croaked.

"Ah...no I think it's an old hot dog."

Phillip didn't even respond right away. What do you say to someone who just found an old wiener in his closet?

"Whizzy. There is really something wrong with you."

"Did you find it?" Rachel yelled as she burst into the room. Aevion the mouse sat on her shoulder. I didn't think it was possible, but his eyes bulged out even more after seeing the disaster in my room.

"Are you referring to his wand or his wie..." Phillip began.

"Shut up, Phillip! Not funny," I snapped, and then smiled as I finished the sentence in my head. It was funny. "I can't remember where I put it. I thought I hid it in here to keep mom from finding it."

"And you, apparently!" Phillip barked. He was becoming unusually cranky.

"You lost your wand?" Rachel was shocked. "How could you be so...so...?"

"Irresponsible?" Phillip added.

"Stupid?" Rachel finished.

"Look! Are you going to help me find my wand or not?"

We split up and continued searching my room. Phillip looked under my bed,

34

Rachel bravely checked in my dresser drawers, and I continued to claw my way through the closet.

"Phillip!" Rachel called in an uncomfortable voice. "I need you to check this one!"

"What's wrong?"

"It's Whizzy's underwear drawer."

I started to laugh. I had finally reached the back of the closet. Sitting in the right corner was a white sock. "I got it!"

Phillip gave a sigh of relief that he wouldn't have to search my underwear drawer.

Rachel and Phillip rushed to my side as I pulled the white sock out and held it up in the air.

"That's a sock, Whizzy!" Rachel crassly remarked.

"Duh!" I simply replied. "I stashed my wand in the sock and hid it in the closet.

"Why?" My best friend asked.

"I really don't remember why!"
Quickly, I removed my wand and tossed the old dusty sock at Phillip. He attempted to dodge it, but the sock landed on his shoulder.

"Ah, Whizzy. Gross! It smells awful." Phillip looked hilarious as he brushed it off his shoulder, and then attempted to smell himself to see if the stink rubbed off on him.

Rachel and I now both had our wands and we were ready to make the journey back to Mistasia. My sister held Aevion the mouse in her hand as we quietly moved through the hallway trying not to wake up our mom. Once we reached the basement I began to feel an excitement overtake me. My heart pumped so hard it felt like it was coming through my chest. I watched Rachel as she held Aevion in her hands and extended him close to the sliding glass door in our basement. It usually led outside into our backyard, but we all waited for it to once again lead us to Mistasia.

Aevion held a small mushroom in his hand. I hadn't noticed it before. He crumbled it up and then tossed the tiny pieces against the glass door.

Just like it had last summer when Sorcerer LaCroiux's evil snake had slammed its tail into the glass, the door magically changed into a swirling portal.

Rachel was the first to enter with Aevion held tightly in one hand and her wand in the other. She was swept inside and quickly disappeared.

Phillip didn't hesitate for a moment. He was off directly behind Rachel.

I took a deep breath. It sounded like a drum was inside my head as my heart continued to pound. Gripping my wand tightly, I sprinted for the portal, leapt into the air and felt a gust of wind pull me in.

A DIFFERENT MISTASIA

7

Traveling in a portal is kind of like riding a roller coaster without the safety straps while flying through the air at great speed, twisting and bouncing. It only lasted for a few seconds... then silence. There was no movement.

My eyes were closed tightly, but I quickly realized that Mistasia would be much different than the last time we visited. I instantly thought about our conversation in the basement a few hours earlier. It was thirteen years in the future here...it would be different.

The ground was strange. I opened my eyes and realized I was lying on my back. The sky was gloomy and full of rough-shaped dark gray clouds. They overlapped each other like pancakes stacked on a plate.

I couldn't see any blue...like the beautiful sky last time we had visited.

"Whizzy?" I heard Rachel calling for me.

I sat up in what used to be a tall green grass field. Now it was covered in deep snow. All around me was white, which made me stick out like a pimple on the big bully, Billy Lawton's, ugly face.

Once again I had transformed into a red-haired fox. Rachel now stood beside me. She was also a fox, but bronze colored. Phillip had changed, too. He was again a green tree frog with long arms and legs and bright red eyes.

"So, it's winter here, too," Phillip said with obvious disappointment in his voice.

I can't imagine that being a frog helps much in the winter. At least Rachel and I have furry coats to keep us warm. I wondered if the snow would make him

39

strong like water did the last time. I guessed
we would find out soon enough.

"Where is Aevion?" Rachel wondered
aloud.

We all searched around not realizing
that he wouldn't still be a small black mouse.
Walking toward us was a shorter than
expected, young dark-skinned boy. He was
even smaller than me. His hair was short
and curly, and he had big, bright green eyes.
I think he's a midget.

"Hurry! Follow me," Aevion spoke and
then quickly darted away in the opposite
direction of Cadieux Castle.

"Where are you going?" I yelled as he
swiftly separated from us. I was shocked at
how fast he was. Everyone here in Mistasia
must be really fast.

He stopped and turned. The snow
almost came to his waist. It looked like he
was sinking. He had a peculiar expression on

his face. Aevion waved his arms urging us to join him.

"Wait!" I yelled to Aevion again. "He's in a hurry!" I crassly remarked to Phillip and Rachel.

When we caught up with him, Aevion explained, "I must take you across Red River and lead you in the direction of The Deadly Spray Forest. There you will meet up with Commander Tallon."

"So, we aren't going to the Castle?" Phillip asked.

"No, Phillip the Frog."

This guy is annoying I thought. He was really starting to bother me. I hoped we wouldn't have to spend much time around him. I might have to use a spell to change him back into a mouse.

Phillip started laughing.

I forgot that in Mistasia he was telepathic and could read our minds. He had just heard everything I thought. Honestly, that kind of bothered me, too.

Rachel looked at Phillip as if he was going crazy. She gave him that what-are-you-laughing-at look that she gave me every day. Usually, it was because I was laughing at something strange that she just didn't find funny.

I pointed at my forehead.

She now gave me the same look.

"Ah forget it...I'll tell you later, Rachel." Ever since we had landed in Mistasia I had become very agitated. My whole body felt wrong...I mean more wrong than the fact that I was a furry red fox with the ability to turn a tree inside out.

"Come on, Whizzy!" suddenly echoed inside my head. Phillip was yelling at me using his 'special' telepathic powers.

I snapped out of my daze just in time to notice Phillip's green-skinned frame disappearing over a hill. Rachel and Aevion were gone too.

I dashed off to catch them.

"Stay out of my head, Phillip," I barked. It didn't take someone with telepathic powers to realize that I was making everyone feel uncomfortable...especially our guide, Aevion.

No one spoke for a while. We trekked through the deep snow. Phillip hopped. Aevion lead the way with Rachel and Phillip right behind, like eager puppies following their master. I, however, was falling further behind. We reached another hill, which was lined with short evergreen trees. When they had ascended to the top, I had just reached the bottom.

"Come on, Whizzy," Rachel urged with a tone that sounded exactly like our mom. "You need to move faster."

I could feel the rage moving through my body. **I'll show you faster.** I thought, knowing that Phillip would hear me. He reached out and pulled Rachel towards him. I held my wand extended above my head, then jabbed it down toward the ground. My body was catapulted into the air. Before they could react, I was standing next to them on top of the hill.

"Fast enough for you, Sis?"

She never answered. I think Phillip told her to ignore me in his 'special' way.

Ahead of us was a small clearing at the bottom of the hill, which was much steeper on the back side. Then, Red River flowed briskly, with sharp rocks sticking out amidst the crashing water in the distance. Only a long, thin bridge stretched over the river for us to cross.

I burst into the air again and landed safely at the bottom. When I turned around, Rachel and Phillip were headed right for me. Trying to run away, I slipped in the powdery snow. Phillip missed me and landed softly to my left. Rachel, however, didn't. She crashed into me and we tumbled through the snow and slid to a stop about twenty feet away. I bolted up.

"You did that on purpose, Rachel!" I growled, but she didn't respond.

"Rachel, are you okay!" Phillip gulped. My tall green friend went to her side without even asking me if I was all right.

Her eyes fluttered for a few seconds as she tried to focus. Then, when she tried to get up, Phillip caught her as she stumbled.

Suddenly, I felt bad for yelling at her. "What were you thinking?" I knew it sounded bad the second I said it, but now the damage was done.

"Lay off, Whizzy," Phillip argued with a strange sound in his voice.

I thought he was going to cry.

"She landed on *me*, Phillip. Stop protecting her," I answered hotly.

"I'm not...she's hurt. Maybe if her brother actually cared I wouldn't have to protect her."

The argument would have lasted longer, but Rachel walked away. Then, Phillip followed.

"Some friend," I muttered aloud.

Aevion had made his way down the steep hillside and joined us mid argument.

"Whizzy is everything all right?" He asked. His eyes felt like they stared into my brain. It was really creepy.

"No, Aevion. My sister and her new best friend are starting to annoy me." I began walking for Red River. At this point, I really didn't care if they followed or not. Grace needed our help, so I was going to find her.

WHY IS IT CALLED RED RIVER?

8

It didn't take very long for me to reach Red River. Only moments later I heard Phillip's voice and this time it echoed through the air instead of my head, which was nice for a change.

"Whizzy! Wait up."

I took a deep breath to calm myself. Fighting with my best friend wasn't something I was good at. It hadn't happened often, but most of them were very recent...since we came back from Mistasia on our first journey.

"Hey, look I'm sorry I yelled, but she didn't mean it," Phillip started to explain when Rachel interrupted.

"Why are you so angry?" She barked.

I could feel the cool breeze against my sharp front teeth as I sneered at her. A deep growl escaped from me.

Phillip croaked, "Whizzy don't!"

It was too late. I roared at her and pounced on top of her. She landed on her back in the snow. Quickly, she kicked me up into the air. I flipped over and landed on all four paws.

Rachel and I stared at each other. I stood on my hind legs again and positioned my wand so it pointed directly between her eyes. She did the same.

"Try it," she dared me.

"What would you like me to turn you into...a slimy slug maybe?"

Rachel growled back, "You're not fast enough, Whizzy. I'll have you buried up to your eyeballs in dirt before you could blink."

Aevion stood paralyzed. He couldn't believe what he saw. Grace had sent him to get us because we were supposed to save

Mistasia, but right now we couldn't save ourselves from...ourselves.

Phillip stood a couple feet behind Rachel. He didn't speak...which made me wonder what he and my sister were plotting against me.

"Shut up, Phillip!" I yelled. "You stay out of it."

"I didn't say anything!" Phillip lied.

"You're talking to her using your telepathy."

"No, I'm not," Phillip tried to defend himself.

"Don't lie! I can see it in her eyes. I can't trust either of you," I screamed.

"You've lost your mind, Whizzy," Rachel said as she slackened her grip on her wand.

Phillip turned his head toward the river. "What was that?"

Aevion scrambled to Phillip's side.

Rachel gave me a scornful glare and then joined them at the edge of the cold rushing riverbank.

I felt of shudder of frustration in my arms as I pulled them to my side. I wasn't going to join them. They were trying to trick me.

"What did you see?" I heard Rachel ask.

"What color was it, Phillip the Frog?" Aevion hastily questioned.

"Color?" I thought.

"It was bright red."

"Was it long and scaly?" Aevion seemed determined to rule out something.

"Yeah!"

"We need to cross the river now!" Aevion screamed and dashed for the narrow wooden structure.

Phillip and Rachel didn't hesitate to follow. The three sped over the bridge and safely reached the other side.

"Come on, Whizzy! Hurry!" Phillip spoke in my head.

"Fine," I replied in disgust. This seemed ridiculous, but I remembered that Mistasia did have the ability to turn ugly in seconds. As I began to cross the narrow bridge, I jogged slightly. I really wasn't in any hurry to join my sister on the other side. She would probably try and turn me into a football and then kick me back across the river.

A loud rushing of water rose up from below me. I slowed down to look over the side. Below was the clearest water I had ever seen. The water was like a pane of glass on an aquarium. Underneath were rocks of all different sizes and colors. Some had green moss growing on them. I could feel, against my fur, the cold air rising off the water. It was soothing. My muscles began to loosen. I felt the grip on my wand lessen. A fish swam out from under the bridge. It whipped its tail vigorously against the current. **Why would it be swimming against the water?** I thought.

Suddenly, a streak of bright red split the river and then disappeared. It left a wake behind. When the water settled, the fish was gone.

I searched around for any sign, but it had vanished.

"Whizzy!" Rachel yelled to me.

"What are you doing?" Aevion screamed. "You must cross the river!" He sounded frantic.

I looked away from the river for a moment. Everything seemed to slow down. I saw them standing at the edge of the bridge pointing up river. When I turned back, I saw a horrifying image.

Jumping out of the water was a bright red giant creature. It looked like a cross between an eel and a fish. Its mouth was wide open. Sharp fangs stuck out

around a slender, pink forked-tongue. I
ducked as the creature flew over the bridge
and gracefully landed in the river on the
other side.

I leapt to my feet and suddenly
realized why this perfectly clear river was
called 'Red'. Names in Mistasia aren't only
descriptive, but important, like Wolverine
Forest...because it's full of angry large
wolverines that are out to kill you. Red River
has a deadly bright red monster that will
try to eat you.

I ran as fast as my fox paws would
take me toward the end of the bridge.
Phillip and Rachel began yelling at me as I
approached, but I couldn't understand them.
They were again pointing, which I knew
meant only bad news so I didn't bother to
look. I didn't really want to...I had already
seen the hideous monster that apparently
craved a large helping of fox for dinner. As I

reached the edge of the bridge I dove for the snow.

Just then the creature crashed into the bridge jarring it loose. It bounced skyward before flopping onto the snowy riverbank. It slid sideways and crashed into a pair of small evergreens. The tree on the left bent over and slowly fell onto the creature. A branch pierced its scaly skin, trapping it.

"Whizzy, are you all right?" Rachel cried as she grabbed me and pulled me off the ground. Five minutes ago she was going to hurt me! Girls...I'll never understand them.

"Come on, before it gets free!" Aevion cried as he ran away.

None of us argued as we quickly followed him away from the river. In the distance, we could hear the creature screeching and thrashing.

I would say that I was glad to be getting away from that situation, but we were now headed directly for The Deadly Spray Forest, which doesn't sound much friendlier than the river we just left behind.

WINTER LASTS HOW LONG?

9

I was furious. Our guide hadn't mentioned the flesh-eating creature lurking in the river. What else was he hiding from us? His secretive manner was similar to Grace's from our last trip. He was reminding me of Grace with each passing hour...just not as pretty.

"When were you gonna tell us about the giant flying monster, Aevion?" I growled as I grabbed him by the arm.

He began cowering and hid his face.

I was shocked to see how frightened of me he had become. I was definitely never feared at Greenville High School. Suddenly, I felt like a bully, and the last thing I wanted was to be like Billy Lawton.

"I'm sorry, Aevion. I didn't mean to...I was just angry. I'm sorry."

Rachel sat down beside Aevion to comfort him. I walked away shaking my head. **How stupid.** I yelled at myself.

"Don't worry about it, Whizzy," Phillip tried to console me. "You've been really upset ever since we got here. What's wrong?"

I struggled to control my thoughts. The last thing I needed now was to fight with my best friend about how much it upset me that he liked my sister. He couldn't help it. Phillip had always liked my sister. I instead thought about Grace.

"Are you worried about Grace?" Phillip responded seconds later. "She will be just fine. She's an elven warrior."

A smile crossed my face. I missed Grace. She was amazing, pretty, strong, and angry. Everything I could ever want in a girl.

"Do you think she's okay, Phillip? Can you see her?" I wanted him to use his powers of clairvoyance to connect with her. Maybe he would be able to find her in his dreams and see if she was safe.

"I can try," Phillip said and then closed his eyes. He stood completely still.

Rachel joined us.

"Is Aevion gonna be okay?" I asked her.

"Yeah. He is really frightened by your anger. He is just sensitive. It's like his body can read your moods somehow. Aevion just knows when you are getting upset, which he said has been almost the entire time in Mistasia." Rachel gave me a motherly glance.

It was creepy how much she looked like mom when she was upset with me. "You look just like mom," I told her.

She smiled.

"No, Rachel, that's not good. Cut it out!"

She smiled even wider. "What is Phillip doing?"

"Trying to contact Grace for me. I asked him to use his powers and see if he could find her in the forest." I turned to look behind us. The Deadly Spray Forest loomed in the distance.

"It's not working, Whizzy," Phillip responded. He sounded distraught.

"Can you talk to her?" I asked.

Phillip tried, but I could tell immediately that he had no response.

"I'm sorry, Whizzy."

Rachel grabbed Phillip's arm. "I'm sure she's fine, Whizzy. She can take care of herself."

"I know." I walked away from the group. The moon began to show through a gap in the clouds. It was dull and colorless. The sun had finally set. It was nighttime in Mistasia...the time I dreaded most. This place was scary enough in the daytime; shadows only made it more terrifying.

It had begun to snow very lightly. Flurries dangled in the air in front of the dark green trees. It was amazingly beautiful. I just wished it were warmer. Even with this fur coat, I felt the stiff winter breeze.

"You're dang right it's cold," Phillip chattered. He had his thin amphibian limbs wrapped around his body in a vain attempt to stay warm. "Hold me, Whizzy." He said in a silly voice.

"I don't think so. You can get Rachel to do that. I'm the best friend...not the girlfriend."

"She's not my girlfriend," Phillip quickly responded.

Neither of us spoke for a moment. Then Phillip added, "I wish she was."

"I know, Phillip." I wasn't going to continue this conversation...although it would have probably started my blood boiling and warmed my body up.

Phillip shuttered as a chill went up his spine. "Darn it!" He yelled out. "I hope it warms up soon."

"Winter has just begun," Aevion's small voice answered.

We all gave him a strange glance.

"He's just wishing for warmer weather. He was kidding, Aevion," I explained.

"Yes, but winter has just begun."

"Right, it started last month," Rachel said meaning November back in Greenville.

Aevion laughed uncomfortably. He sounded like a child's squeaky toy. Then, he began to explain, "Last month. You are very funny, Rachel the Wizard Fox. It has been winter for over a year."

"A year?" Rachel, Phillip and I said in surprised unison.

"How is that possible?" Winter is only a quarter of the year. A little more than three months...from December through

March," Phillip pleaded with Aevion as if he was going to change his mind on how long the winters in Mistasia were.

"I am sorry, Phillip the Frog, but winters here last for six years."

"What?" Phillip croaked.

"Six years!" I was floored. The winters in Greenville were pretty brutal...cold winds, heavy snow and freezing temperatures, but at least it only lasted for a couple months. Then, it would warm up and summer made us forget about how miserable the winters were.

"That's awful." Rachel sounded like she was going to cry.

I immediately imagined her trapped in an igloo, frozen solid with some dumb look on her face. Phillip punched me in the shoulders and then did some weird eye-blinking thing.

"What was that?" I laughed while rubbing my shoulder. I don't even think

Phillip realized that his eyes were blinking independently but it was creepy.

"That's rude," Phillip responded referring to my image of Rachel frozen in the igloo. I really needed to control my thoughts around him.

Is six years of winter even possible? I thought.

"What?" Phillip responded.

"Will you cut that out? I am going to turn you into something that doesn't talk!" I barked.

"Whizzy, be quiet," Rachel demanded.

She was trying to figure something out in her head. I could always tell, because she would crinkle up her nose and furrow her eyebrows. It made her look really angry. It must be what I look like all the time.

Finally, she blurted out, "That sounds about right."

"What are we talking about?" I questioned. The last thing I was talking about was her being trapped in an igloo, but I was fairly certain that she wasn't in the same frame of mind...so I figured I'd ask.

"Remember we did the math and it had been about thirteen years here in Mistasia since we had left?"

Phillip and I both nodded.

"The math works out. It would mean that each year in Greenville would be approximately twenty-four years here! Each season lasts about one quarter of the year back home, so it must work the same way here. Therefore, winter or summer or whatever season would last six years!"

"That's ridiculous!" I blurted out.

"She's correct, Whizzy," My best friend said siding again with my sister.

"Well, I guess we're in for a long journey," I added as the snow began to increase.

"We had better get moving. It is only another ten miles to The Deadly Spray Forest," Aevion, our guide, urged.

ARE YOU GONNA GET SICK?
10

Each breath expelled from my mouth like a winding snake slithering out and curling up into a strange-knotted mess. The temperature in Mistasia had dropped quite a bit in the last hour. My whiskers drooped down under the weight of the icicles that had formed around my mouth. Snow had clumped up in my fur. I had white blotches all over my body as the snow attacked me.

Rachel looked the same. Phillip didn't have any snow on him at all. In fact he appeared to shine in the moonlight. As the sun completely disappeared, the once dull colorless moon had exploded. It was bright and large in the sky when it peaked between clouds like the eye of some ever-present creature watching us move through the snow. That light reflected off of Phillip's skin and glowed. The snow was melting against his skin and turning into water, which kept his froggy legs strong. It was another one of Phillip's powers here in Mistasia...water against his amphibian skin gave him extreme strength.

The snow had fallen harder with each passing moment. In the distance, The Deadly Spray Forest slowly disappeared from view. Now, before us, was a blur of white.

"Aevion, how much farther?" I yelled.

All I heard was a mumbled response as the small dark-skinned boy struggled through the deep snow, which had now reached his waist. If it were much longer, he would be buried alive.

"What?" I shouted back.

"It should be just up ahead," Phillip responded in my head.

It startled me. You think I would be used to that by now.

Then, like walking under an umbrella, the snow cascaded off the branches of a thirty-foot tall tree. As I walked underneath the snowdrifts became very small, only a few inches deep.

I looked to the sky and saw the skinny tree's trunk twist and turn into the air. It bent near the top at a strange angle like it was attempting to straighten itself. Then, almost at the top of the tree was the umbrella-like top. The branches were more like vines that intertwined and locked to form knots. Each group of branches also had thick carpet-like bushes sprouting from them. Even though some snow flurries leaked through, the trees created a roof over the forest floor. Now, for the first time since we arrived back in Mistasia, I could see the ground in some spots.

"Creepy," My sister said. "It's so quiet in here."

When looking into The Deadly Spray Forest it was like a series of saltshakers had been turned upside down as small amounts of snow trickled through the thick, dense tree cover and sprinkled onto the ground below in little circles.

"We are here," Aevion announced.

He didn't seem very comfortable with that either.

"What next?" Phillip asked our guide.

"I am not certain, Phillip the Frog. I was only supposed to bring you to the forest. This was the meeting point," Aevion nervously explained. It was obvious that he expected Grace to be here waiting for us.

"Phillip, try to talk to her," I said. He was able to speak to Grace through telepathy, something the elves in Mistasia shared with my best friend.

Phillip's big circular red eyes disappeared behind his green frog eyelids. He stood completely still for only a few moments. Then, he began to sway like a gust of wind pushed against him, but the air was completely still in The Deadly Spray Forest. Next, his face began to contort and he started to mumble like he was having a nightmare. Suddenly, he crumpled to the ground and landed in a heap.

"Phillip," Rachel screamed and rushed to his side.

I joined her, and we helped Phillip sit up.

When he opened his big red eyes he looked dizzy.

"Are you gonna throw up?" I asked him. Believe me, I have seen that look before and it almost always ended in Phillip barfing.

"Whizzy!" Rachel scolded. "He's not gonna throw up...are you, Phillip?" She didn't sound as confident after looking into his eyes which starting rolling back into his head.

Aevion stood completely silent directly behind us. He just anxiously watched to see what would happen next.

"What did you see, Phillip? Is Grace in danger? Is she okay?" I urged him to answer, but he just couldn't get any words to come out.

Phillip struggled to move his mouth. The last time I saw him like this I had accidentally hit him in the head with a soccer ball in my backyard. And yes...he threw up that time.

We spent a couple more minutes trying to pry information out of him, but no luck. Then, Aevion stepped up between my sister and me. He just placed his hand in front of Phillip's face and snapped his fingers.

"Grace!" Phillip croaked.

Aevion backed away quickly. Rachel and I did, too.

Phillip gasped for air like he had just come up from underwater. Then, he swallowed before calming himself down.

"Grace is in trouble. Something has her."

Phillip was afraid. That was the look I saw on Phillip Harper's face for as long as I had known him. He was afraid of a lot of things, but as Phillip the Frog I had never seen him so terrified.

"Where is she?" I demanded as I stood up and gripped my wand tightly.

Rachel grabbed my wrist, "Calm down."

"Grace needs our help, Rachel! That's why we are here." I was revved up. A surge of adrenaline shot through my furry body. The hairs on the back of my neck stood up like an electrical charge built up inside me. "Where is she, Phillip?" I demanded again.

"Whizzy, there is something evil in this forest." Phillip looked pale for a guy that was green. The color in his face had faded.

For a moment I could see Phillip Harper from Greenville emerge. He was shaken and scared.

"We are the saviors of Mistasia, Phillip...remember? Grace sent Aevion to find us! Not bring an elven army or creatures from Mistasia...you and me." I reminded my best friend.

"Me, too," Rachel added.

I looked at her for a moment then replied, "Yeah, I know." I was trying to forget that part. "Wherever Phillip is...I'll find you, too." Rachel seemed hurt by my jab, but I didn't care at the moment. This was about saving Grace. "Now, where is she, Phillip?"

I could see how reluctant my best friend was, but he fought against his fear and began running deeper into the forest. I dashed after him with Rachel and Aevion trailing behind me.

SHRIEKING IN THE DEADLY SPRAY FOREST

11

You know that feeling you get after you've made a bad choice? You know that sinking feeling in the pit of your stomach followed by the obvious reaction of wishing you hadn't done whatever it was that you just did?

Well, I had that exact feeling about three minutes after I started to run deeper into The Deadly Spray Forest.

I caught up to Phillip quickly. We ran side by side. Rachel and Aevion were still behind us. We ran between two tangled trees, each of which stood over forty-feet tall. I passed through first with Phillip directly behind me.

I'm not sure if I had ever said these words before in my life, but it just slipped out.

"Holy mother of crap!"

Phillip didn't say anything recognizable. It kind of sounded like his mouth began to speak a foreign tongue. I'd repeat it for you, but I wouldn't come close. Just understand it didn't make any sense at all. My statement had pretty much summed it up.

Rachel burst from between the trees and skidded to a stop. The three of us now stood in a small clearing within the forest.

Inside was a village. Small huts made of bark, wood and sticks were hanging in the air from the trees...dozens of them. That wasn't the most unbelievable part.

Across the clearing was a tall, thin and yellowish-looking creature. Its bony body dangled upside down in the tree next to a hut. It had black eyes and no nose, just two small holes. Its ears were round and floppy. Suddenly, I noticed these things were everywhere.

Maybe they're elves. I hoped.

I could hear shrieking and scratching. Then, I noticed a few other traits. These creatures had claws where they should have hands. Suddenly, one of them reached its arms above its hairy head, exposing wings that attached to their elbows and sides. It jumped from the tree and swooped down slightly before climbing into the air and landing in a nearby tree.

"That thing just flew," Rachel whispered.

We all began to walk backwards. Somehow, we hadn't been noticed.

My heart was pounding like a drum. It thumped so loudly that I swore one of those creatures could hear it. I placed my hands over my chest in a silly attempt to quiet my pounding heart.

"What in the world are those?" Phillip asked. His mouth was wide open in shock.

"Vampire bats," Aevion responded in a quiet yet blunt tone.

"You have to be joking?" I blurted out still holding my chest. "Are they good or bad?" I added.

"They look bad," Rachel quickly responded.

"Shh!" Phillip was frightened as a vampire bat swooped past directly in front of us. It shrieked an awful sound that hurt my ears. "Bats have great hearing."

"Actually, these vampire bats are not much different from elves, Phillip the Frog. They do have good hearing, but it's unidirectional." Aevion explained.

"What does that mean?" I asked.

"They won't be able to hear unless you are talking in their direction. If you are facing away from where the vampire bats are, their ears won't hear your sound waves.

However, if you speak, even at a whisper, in their direction...they will hear you."

"Whizzy these creatures have Grace!" Phillip spoke to me using his 'special' powers.

I hadn't really mastered the way to respond back without speaking out loud yet, so I nodded instead. With my wand in hand, I stood up and started back into the clearing through the twisted trees.

Aevion reached out and grasped my wrist, "Don't attack them, Whizzy. They won't hurt you."

I gave him a quizzical glance. **If they won't hurt me than why are we hiding from them?** I thought.

"Good question," I heard in my head. Phillip stood next to me with a smirk on his big green face. His two large red eyes gazed at me. I hadn't realized until now just how large his eyes were. They were bigger than the headlights on my parents' car.

"Then, why are we hiding?" I finally asked.

"I don't know, Whizzy the Wizard Fox. You and your friends were standing here when I arrived," Aevion replied.

"Oh!" I didn't know what else to say.

I peeked back through the trees and noticed a group of vampire bats flying in a circle directly overhead. They appeared to be playing. One would screech and then they would dart off in different directions, as one vampire bat would chase them. I watched curiously as it chased down another vampire bat and jumped on its back. These two began to scuffle with each other, biting and clawing at one another while falling toward the forest floor. At the last moment, they separated and flew back up into another circle. The whole thing started again.

"I think they are playing some game," I announced to Rachel, Phillip and Aevion, who all stood behind the trees.

They followed me into the clearing again. This time it didn't take long for them to notice us. Quickly, three vampire bats descended upon us. They landed in front of us. Vampire bats may be thin, but they are quite tall. Phillip only came to their chests and he was over six-feet tall. Their faces were hideous. Now that they stood on their feet, their ears drooped back and their faces appeared wrinkled. They looked like they were hundreds of years old.

"Can they talk, Aevion?" I asked our guide.

"I'm not certain," he replied as he hid behind Phillip.

My heart was racing again. Aevion had said that they wouldn't hurt us, but I had my doubts. He had also conveniently forgotten to explain the eel-fish in Red River; maybe he forgot that vampire bats were bad.

I summoned up the courage to speak. "Do you know where Grace Tallon is?"

The three vampire bats looked at one another, but didn't make a sound. Suddenly, the creature on the right noticed my wand and shrieked. Dozens of his brethren in the trees took to flight in the forest.

I asked again, "Grace Tallon...have you seen her?

The tallest of the three vampire bats bent over and stuck his scary face in mine before responding, "Who are you and why have you entered our forest?"

VOICE IN THE SHADOWS

12

The vampire bats grizzly voice was followed by the most disgusting smell. It was like sweaty feet and cooked spinach. My stomach gurgled, and I felt myself getting sick. This wouldn't be very good if I barfed all over him.

"Wow, that breath's awful."

I heard Rachel and Phillip gasp behind me, and I suddenly realized that I had just said that out loud.

The vampire bat's face crumpled in anger. He stood upright again and shrieked.

Before I could realize what was happening, the vampire bats snatched the three of us off the ground and leapt into the air.

I struggled to free myself from his bony claws until I saw how far above the forest floor we were. My red and black fox legs dangled in the air.

We flew high into the air and then dipped down. My stomach flipped like on a roller coaster. Then, we did a complete spin like we were trapped in a washing machine. I was certainly glad that I hadn't eaten lately.

Phillip and Rachel were right behind us. The vampire bats flew to the end of the clearing and headed straight for a tangled group of trees.

"Oh no!" I yelled as it looked like this vampire bat was going to crash us into them. At the last second, he tilted sideways and slipped through a gap. It was dark, but I could hear the trees whizzing past us at great speed. A small sliver of light was up ahead. It grew wider and taller each second until it opened up into a large room.

The vampire bat swooped across the wooden floor and let me go. I hit the floor and slid into the wall.

"Ouch!" I yelled as I hit my paw against the hard wall. Then, I heard Phillip and Rachel screaming.

They were flying through the air right at me. Phillip bounced on his rear, flew over me, and landed face first into the wall. He slithered to the floor like a snake. Rachel landed on her side and began rolling toward me. I jumped to avoid her, but she clipped my legs and knocked me on top of her. The three of us rested in a heap. I struggled to keep my eyes open as the room spun. Rachel and Phillip were both out cold. It wasn't long before I joined them.

When I awoke, my head was throbbing. A dull noise echoed in my ears. Rachel was still passed out lying on her stomach. Phillip was laying over her in a painfully awkward fashion. His legs were underneath Rachel, but his body was bent backwards over her like a pretzel. I checked them to make sure they were both still breathing.

"They are alive, Whizzenmog." A familiar voice rang out.

I struggled to find where it was coming from. The room still moved uncontrollably in my vision. From my hands and knees, I crawled away from my sister and best friend.

"Where are you going?" The voice laughed. His voice seemed to be coming from everywhere, like I was inside it.

I slowly felt the room begin to stop moving. The pounding in my head had ended. After taking a deep breath, I pushed myself to my feet. Stumbling backwards I crashed to the ground again. Dizziness had trounced me. From my back, I noticed there was no ceiling in this room, just darkness. I rolled to my side and again attempted to stand up.

"You are persistent," The voice mocked me. I could recognize it. It was hateful and mean. Laughing again he said, "I could watch you struggle forever, but that would be a waste of valuable time. Pick him up!" He barked in a deeper tone.

The vampire bat's claws gripped me once again and picked me off the ground. Hanging in the air, fear began to take over. I struggled to loosen its grasp, but the creature was much too strong.

That is when I realized that my wand was gone. I had dropped it when the vampire bat had thrown me into the room. I was helpless. I felt like I was back in Greenville fighting a schoolyard bully.

My vision had become much better, but I still couldn't see where the voice was coming from. The room looked empty.

Torches lit the room along the wall, which was round and brown.

We must be inside a tree trunk. I thought.

"Do you remember me, Whizzenmog?" His voice taunted me.

"No!" I replied. **Phillip, wake up!** I tried to reach my friend. Hopefully, he would wake up and hear me. **Phillip, wake up!** I said in my mind.

"You really don't remember me?" The voice asked again. Suddenly, his face appeared before me out of darkness.

"Ah!" I screamed. "LaCroiux!"

Standing before me was Sorcerer Pierre LaCroiux.

"The last time I saw you King Cragon had banished you from the castle," I added.

"Yes! I guess that would be the last time you would remember." LaCroiux looked even older than before. His eyes were sunken deep into his skinny skull. Black circles surrounded them, swallowing up the whites of his eyes. It was frightening to look at. It almost looked like his eyes were missing. His white beard was even longer than before, but still braided. It looked like an icicle hanging from his chin.

"I was banished because of you and your sister. My king punished me because I failed to get rid of you two," LaCroiux began to explain.

"He isn't king anymore, LaCroiux!" I growled. The longer I was being held the angrier I was becoming. My frustration was setting in.

"Yes. I guess it seems you took care of that too." He just stared at me with those blank eyes. "It has been thirteen years since you defeated me. I have been waiting for the king to return to power, hoping that he would forgive me...take me back."

"That will never happen!" Rachel suddenly bellowed from behind me. She had both wands in her paws. "Let him go!" She demanded.

The vampire bat placed me back on solid ground, but refused to let go.

"Well, it appears we meet again, Rachel and Michael Whizzenmog...the last wizards of Mistasia. You do realize that while you were away, sorcery increased its popularity in these lands. Cadieux Castle is becoming weaker. Soon, your queen will no longer be in power," Sorcerer LaCroiux explained.

"Not if we have anything to say about it," Rachel retorted while raising her wand toward the sorcerer's heart. "We'll stop you just like we stopped your precious king."

"Ah...ah...ah, my dear, I wouldn't do that if I were you." LaCroiux said in a fatherly tone. "You have no idea what you are involved in, child. This isn't a game. Lives are at risk."

Rachel stepped forward and LaCroiux suddenly disappeared into a mist. She angrily pointed her wand at the vampire bat holding me prisoner.

"Let go!" She vented.

It shrieked and exposed its fangs, but then backed away.

"This will not end well, Whizzenmogs. I promise you both that," LaCroiux's voice echoed.

Rachel tossed me my wand. Phillip now awoke and joined us. The three of us stood in the middle of the wooden room, back to back, searching for any sign of LaCroiux.

"What's going on? What are we looking for?" Phillip requested.

"It's Sorcerer LaCroiux!" I answered.

"He's back?" Phillip croaked. "That can't be good." I could hear his stomach flip. That's the Phillip I knew, uncomfortable and afraid.

"Show yourself, you coward," I growled.

Suddenly, LaCroiux's face appeared before me. "BOO!" He yelled.

I flicked my wrist and shot a white bolt of lightning out of my wand. Just then his face disappeared and the bolt slammed into the wall. It scorched the wood, which smoldered.

"I have a present for you!" He laughed. "Follow the light, Whizzenmogs."

"It's a trap, Whizzy," Rachel urged.

"I know."

"Whizzy, Grace is here," Phillip said trying to remind me why we were here.

I began to walk down a slim hallway. As I walked, it felt like the walls were closing in on me. Rachel and Phillip followed, but so did the vampire bat. It stalked slowly, following Phillip. When I reached the end, there was another small room. The ceiling was very low and the area was no larger than Phillip's bedroom in Greenville.

Once inside I stopped. I could hear mumbling, but no one was there. Rachel stood beside me. Phillip bumped into me, almost knocking me down, as he backed into the room. The tall hideous creature creeping up behind him kept him preoccupied. The vampire bat stopped just outside the room.

Suddenly, I had a sinking feeling in my gut. Again, I heard a mumbled voice call out.

"Grace?" Phillip responded and then he turned around.

Right in front of us was Grace Tallon and Aevion. She had her mouth covered with some sort of clear paste that kept her from talking. Aevion looked terrified and had his hands behind his back.

Then, a loud bang echoed from behind me. The door had closed. I turned and fired a spell at it, but nothing happened. We were trapped.

I FELT SOMETHING FOOLISH
COMING ON
13

"I told you it was a trap!" Rachel yelled. "Darn you, Whizzy." She frantically looked to find any way to open the door. "I can't find it!" She shouted.

"What?" Phillip replied. "How can that be? Whizzy, there is no door!"

"It's black magic...evil and treacherous." Aevion replied. "You can't escape."

"Watch me," I boasted. I walked over to where the door had been; motioned Rachel and Phillip to move aside and readied my wand.

"Your magic won't work! You cannot escape this room." LaCroiux's voice boomed. "I have been waiting for this moment. Never did I believe that it would be so easily accomplished, but thankfully you aren't as smart as everyone believed," Sorcerer LaCroiux sneered.

A pale-skinned hand poked through the wall where the door had been as if the wall wasn't even there.

I heard Phillip gasp with astonishment. Then, he mumbled something. I couldn't understand him, but I'm sure it wasn't good.

The hand easily moved through the solid wooden wall, followed by an arm and then Sorcerer LaCroiux's ugly, sagging face. He almost looked like the vampire bat creatures. When LaCroiux had completely stepped through the wall, his minion followed.

"How is that possible?" I blurted out. "Are you a ghost?" I added. After I said it, I wished that I hadn't because it sounded like a dumb question.

LaCroiux just smiled. He was completely enjoying every minute of this. It was like he had been planning this exact moment for the past thirteen years and now he was so satisfied he couldn't help but gloat.

"No, I am certainly alive, Whizzenmog," His reply was in a patronizing tone.

I could feel a division in the room, like a line was drawn on the floor. Phillip, Aevion, my sister and I stood on one side all wondering what was to happen next, while Sorcerer Pierre LaCroiux and his vampire bat stood on the other daring us to try and escape. He was challenging us...the saviors of Mistasia...without even saying a word.

"Whizzy, what do we do?" Phillip whispered into my ear.

What could we do? I wondered to myself. Grace was the strategist. She would have a plan...GRACE!

97

I darted around and startled Phillip.
Pushing past Aevion I looked for Grace, but
she was gone. There was no trace of her.

"But she was just here!" I shouted.

"Who?" Aevion questioned.

"Grace," I started when LaCroiux
rudely interjected.

"Ah yes, my boy. Grace Tallon.
Another one of Queen Merran Cadieux's
great warriors."

A surge of warm blood began to boil
in my chest. I could literally feel it moving
through my veins and entering my entire
body. My legs and arms began to swell with
hatred. Frustration had always been one of
my biggest weaknesses...it always forced me
to do foolish things. Right now, I felt
something foolish coming on.

When I turned to face our enemy, I
caught a single glimpse of a smile on
Aevion's small mousey face. He hadn't come
close to smiling at any point in our journey.

Since I had known him, he had shown nothing but fear. Why would he be smiling at the very moment I was about to explode and start a battle? Why wasn't he afraid now?

"Whizzy!" I heard Grace's voice leap into my head. She was using her elven abilities to contact me. She hadn't ever done that before. That was something only her and Phillip shared.

During this whole time while my foxy mind was wondering, Sorcerer LaCroiux had been babbling on. Right about now, I felt the sudden urge to shut him up!

"LaCroiux!" I yelled. "Release us!"

He cocked his head sideways and growled, "Make me."

Suddenly, the room was ablaze with wands and sorcery. Phillip dashed to the corner grabbing Aevion along the way.

Rachel and I attacked the sorcerer from two sides. He was very powerful, even more than I remembered. Blasts of color zapped from the tip of my wand.

LaCroiux knelt down and ran his hand across the floor like he was drawing a line. He snapped his arm upward and the floor cracked and bent, forming a wooden shield. My spells harmlessly splashed against it like watercolor paints on paper.

Rachel attempted to freeze him just as we had King Cragon Cadieux, but Sorcerer LaCroiux was expecting that. He produced a flame from his pocket. It lunged toward Rachel and collided with her freezing spell. When they touched, it produced a violent reaction. Thick smoke filled the room.

Everyone stood completely still for a moment. An evil laugh eerily pierced the silence. A stream of light sliced through the smoke like a sword cutting it in half. Then the light spread out and tore the cloud of smoke apart into opposite corners of the room, and in the middle stood our enemy.

"You will have to do better than that," He sneered and then stepped forward slamming his foot on the ground. It shook the room knocking Rachel and me to the floor.

A shrieking sound blasted out from next to me. The vampire bat now stood over me, and it looked angry...much angrier than normal. It spread its wings and began to reach out for me.

I went to hit it with a spell, when a green foot flashed across my face. It smashed into the vampire bat's chest and sent it disappearing into the smoke.

"Phillip!"

My best friend had just saved my rear.

"That was awesome, Phillip."

We both knew what we had to do next. Rachel was in trouble. The sorcerer had backed her into a corner. She did everything she could to fight him off, but he had become too powerful since we last fought him.

Phillip just snapped. He leapt across the room and landed on LaCroiux's back. Covering the sorcerer's eyes allowed my sister to escape. It wasn't long before Phillip was shaken off. He bounced across the floor and crashed into the wall. I saw him try to get up and then fall flat on his stomach.

LaCroiux just glared at me and smirked. He slowly glided toward us. His robes covered his feet so it appeared as if he was hovering in the air. When he approached us, LaCroiux stopped just a few feet away.

"This will have to wait until another time, Whizzenmogs. I have another matter to attend to," he said before standing up straight. The smoke in the room cleared.

From behind, two vampire bats grabbed Rachel and me. They had snuck up behind us during our battle. Each managed to pry our wands away from us.

"Don't worry! I will come back and finish you both, but for now I will leave you here with my friends." He pointed to the two vampire bats that held us captive. "You haven't had the opportunity to be properly introduced. I figure now is the time, since you will be spending all of it with them until I return. Rachel and Michael Whizzenmog, meet Goren and Vella. They are the rulers of The Deadly Spray Forest."

Before either of us could say anything Sorcerer Pierre LaCroiux disappeared through the wall in a blur of light and was gone.

14

Leaning against the wall in defeat I slowly slid to the floor. I hated to lose at anything, but this wasn't a game. This was real...the queen was in danger. We were all in danger.

I felt the energy leaving my body and was upset with myself for allowing LaCroiux to get away, for allowing us to become trapped in this room and mostly for losing my wand to these ugly creatures.

My head was buried between my furry knees. Staring at the floor, I heard a whimper. For a split second, I thought it was Phillip. When I lifted my head, he was sitting next to me holding onto Rachel. He looked upset, but wasn't crying, and neither was Rachel.

Where is that coming from? I thought.

"I don't know," Phillip responded.
"Do you always have to be up there?
It's not a garage sale you know. My brain
isn't free for you to play around in, so stop
poking around!" I snapped.
"Whizzy, calm down. Phillip isn't
hurting anything," Rachel began to defend
him.
"I'm tired of him in my head. It's
already messed up enough; I don't need him
driving me crazy."
"Fine! I'll stop talking to you, Whizzy."
"Good!" I yelled back.
"Fine!" He yelled back.
"Great!" I growled.
Rachel gave me the mom glare and
shook her head at me. I knew I was wrong
to yell at Phillip, but I was just so sick of
him using his 'special' powers on me. It was
creepy to constantly hear someone else's
voice in my head. It made me feel like I was
going crazy, and I didn't need any help

when I was in Mistasia...here, I always felt like I was crazy!

I must have been exhausted, because before I realized who was crying I was fast asleep. Dreams to me are useless. I almost never remember them, and when I do, they are always crazy. For example... one time I was dreaming about flying through the air as a pop tart, specifically a frosted strawberry pop tart. I had no arms or legs just eyes, at least I think, because I could see. I was flying over a lake of milk, and when I finally crossed it, there were orange and purple cows dancing without music. When I woke up, I understood why. I had fallen asleep in the basement with the television on. In my hand, was a frosted strawberry pop tart and all over my shirt was the milk I had been drinking. I'm still not sure where the colorful cows fit in.

However, tonight was much different. I found myself having the most intense dream of my life. The room was spinning. It stopped and in the corner I saw Grace. She was unable to speak at first, but then her voice began to echo in my head. It was so loud. Her words were muffled, and then became so loud she sounded like a broken speaker crackling and buzzing. I felt like I was floating in the room. I tried to yell for her to stop, but nothing came out. Suddenly, all noise ended. It was scary. I got chills up my spine, like I had just seen a ghost. Then, I heard her speak, "Whizzy, help me!"

I startled awake. My body shook, and I fell to my side. My large fox ear was against the wood floor. The banging of a large drum pulsed in my ear. It took me a second to realize that the banging was my heart against my chest.

Phillip and Rachel had shocked expressions on their faces.

In the opposite corner Aevion sat crying. It had been him I heard whimpering earlier. Beside him were Goren and Vella, the vampire bats. They hadn't moved since LaCroiux had left.

I tried to gather myself.

Phillip kept his word and refused to speak to me. Rachel, however, blurted out one question, "What the heck is wrong with you?"

That was the sister that I had known...before Mistasia. I struggled to stand up. My legs wobbled and my head swam. I felt so dizzy. I mustered the strength to get to my feet and yelled, "Grace!" Something was really wrong with me. I started to fall over when Phillip grabbed hold of my arms.

"Jerk," He simply said.

"Hi, Phillip," I replied. "I need to sit down."

Phillip carefully placed me back on the ground.

"Phillip, Grace is still here. I saw her in my dream.

"This isn't like the pop tart cow dream is it, Whizzy?" Phillip crassly responded. I had forgotten that I told him about that.

I could tell he was still upset with me. "No. There was something real about this dream. Like nothing I had ever felt before. I think Grace was calling to me. She was calling for my help." I attempted to explain but started to wonder if I really was going crazy.

"Why hasn't she contacted me, Whizzy? She could just as easily talk to me."

Phillip was right. Grace hadn't contacted him. It would be easy for her to speak to him. They shared the same ability. Maybe Sorcerer LaCroiux was playing a trick on me.

"No!" Aevion's small mousy voice crackled from across the room. "You are not crazy, Whizzy the Wizard Fox." The fear in Aevion's eyes had returned. He was shaking with it now.

The vampire bats, Goren and Vella, began to make strange noises toward the small dark-skinned boy.

Aevion cringed.

"Leave him alone," Rachel yelled. She stood up and ran to him.

The second she placed her arms around Aevion the vampire bats began to shriek and howl. Goren spread his wings, which looked like they belonged on a jet. Vella's claw-like hands clicked as she tapped her razor sharp fingers together.

"Release him," Goren demanded. "He does not belong to you, wizard." Goren puffed up his chest and opened up his wings to their fullest in an attempt to intimidate Rachel.

Aevion suddenly pushed her away and scurried back toward Goren before sitting on the floor next to him. He placed his head between his knees and covered his face with his arms.

Phillip shook his head in amazement. He couldn't understand what was happening.

"Why do you keep frightening him? He is just a child. Leave him alone?" Rachel defiantly barked at the vampire bats.

"Whizzy, I'm in here," Grace's voice shot into the room for everyone to hear.

"Grace where are you?" I shouted.

"I am here."

"Where is 'here'?" Phillip questioned with a frustrated tone.

"Hidden from sight by LaCroiux's powers," she answered.

Goren and Vella began making noises again. They seemed to be trying to cancel out her voice.

I covered my ears to block their painful sounds.

"Ahhhh!" Phillip screamed. "That's it." He just snapped. My best friend hopped across the room in one leap and attacked. Rachel bravely joined him even without her wand that Vella held in her clutches. I couldn't believe what I was watching and stood motionless.

Phillip dodged a swing from Goren and hopped in the air, landing on the floor behind the nasty creature. When Goren turned to face Phillip, a green webbed foot smacked him in the chin and knocked him down.

Rachel must have realized that she was defenseless against Vella without her wand about five seconds after she confronted the bony beast. Rachel was amazing as she maneuvered her way out of getting clobbered. She ducked and dodged a series of swings from Vella's claws. Then,

Phillip jumped into the air and landed squarely on the vampire bat's back knocking our wands loose and into the air. Rachel dove and caught hers. Mine landed on the floor and rolled directly to me. It stopped against my left foot.

I reached down and grabbed it. A swell of power came over me. Just as I looked up, Rachel finished off Vella with a freezing spell. Goren was next. My sister gracefully spun on her toes like a ballerina. When she stopped, Rachel was in a dancer's pose with her wand extended at Goren. She fired, hitting him in the chest. Now both of our captors were frozen solid, in motion, like a stone statue.

Aevion screamed, "No! Let them go. Leave my parents alone!"

VAMPIRE PARENTS

15

Aevion was crying as he caressed Vella's frozen face. She looked frightening. Her mouth was open wide with her fangs jutting out. Her eyes bulged from their sockets.

We all stood motionless. Our mouths hung open in shock.

"Did he say parents?" Phillip questioned as his voice cracked.

Aevion didn't respond. He just sobbed. Rachel reached out and placed her paw on his shoulder, but Aevion shook it off.

"These aren't your parents, Aevion," Rachel tried to explain. She must have thought he was just confused. "They can't be. You are an elf." She looked at him with pity. His back was still turned toward her.

Finally, Aevion gathered himself long enough to speak, "She is my mother, Rachel the Wizard Fox. They are my parents."

Aevion turned around. He looked different. His eyes had changed. Aevion's entire body began to change shape. Suddenly, standing before us was a small childlike vampire bat-a miniature version of Goren and Vella.

Rachel gasped and stepped backward, bumping into Phillip. He yelped as Rachel stepped on his webbed foot.

"No way!" I recalled saying. "You were one of them the whole time."

We had been fooled, tricked by LaCroiux into believing that Grace had sent Aevion to bring us back to Mistasia in order to help her, but he was setting up a trap here in The Deadly Spray Forest the entire time. Grace knew nothing about us coming back. She was bait for the trap.

I gripped my wand so tightly that I thought it might splinter and break in my paw. I felt so stupid.

"Why did you trick us, Aevion? WHY?" I barked.

The small vampire bat recoiled and hid behind his frozen mother. His beady little eyes and one droopy ear peeked out from her side.

"Answer me. Why are you working with him?"

This time Rachel didn't protect him. She looked just as angry as I did. Raising her wand in the air, she gritted her teeth and said, "Speak or you'll join your parents."

"I...I had no choice. Please don't hurt me." Aevion started to sob again.

Rachel lowered her wand, but I raised mine.

"Whizzy," She said with a sympathetic tone in her voice.

I wouldn't even look in her direction. I was too angry to forgive him. I so badly wanted to zap him with a spell right now.

"I'm sorry, Whizzy the Wizard Fox. I had no choice. He had my parents. He said he would let them go if I went to get you from your world," Aevion stammered between sobs.

I lowered my wand slightly. "Let them go?" I didn't understand. "What do you mean, 'Let them go', Aevion?"

"He has them under his dark magic," Aevion explained.

"Sorcerer LaCroiux is controlling them?" Phillip asked.

Aevion nodded his head from behind his mother.

"Dark magic," Rachel said to me as she grabbed my arm holding my wand and pushed it to my side.

I didn't stop her. She was right. Aevion was being tricked, too. Sorcerer

LaCroiux was using all of us against each other.

"Aevion, where is Grace?" I asked, hoping he knew where Sorcerer LaCroiux was hiding her.

"I do not know," He continued to cry. "My parents might know."

I shot my wand back in his direction.

"Whizzy, don't," Rachel screamed.

"Don't try to trick me," I stared him in the eyes. Then, I tried to contact Phillip without speaking. **Is he lying, Phillip?** I questioned.

"I don't know. She could know, but I have no way to ask her while she is under this spell," Phillip said.

I directed, "Rachel, free Vella only."

Rachel stepped toward Vella and raised her wand.

"Wait!" I demanded. "If this is a trick, Aevion, you will regret it. Only release Vella.

After she takes us to Grace, then we will free Goren."

Rachel hesitated, "Uh...how do we know that they aren't still under LaCroiux's power?" She looked to me for an answer.

We all looked to Aevion.

"I will talk to her. I have changed so maybe she changed, too."

"Right. Okay then...here it goes." Rachel fired a counter spell, freeing Vella.

The mother vampire bat was very angry. She lashed out as if we were still in the battle from earlier.

We all backed away and lowered our wands as Aevion jumped in front of us.

"Mother!" He yelled with tears streaked across his pale face.

Vella's anger seemed to melt away when she saw her son. "Aevion?" She reached out and grabbed him. "You have returned." She sounded different...happy.

Aevion explained to Vella our deal. We would free Goren if she told us how to find Grace. Holding her son tightly, she whispered to him. They both spoke in their vampire bat shrieking tones before Vella turned to me and answered.

"She is in the far corner hidden by shadow. The sorcerer has many tricks wizard. It is in the eyes this time." She pointed behind us into the darkest corner of the room.

I dashed over with my heart racing. I called out for Grace. Muffled noises bounced against the walls. It was so hard to find where they came from.

"Whizzy, she said something about eyes, right?" Phillip said as he searched around the seemingly empty room.

"Yes. 'It is in the eyes this time'. That was what she said," I turned back to see if Vella was trying to attack us from behind.

She and Aevion knelt in front of Goren. It appeared they were praying.

"Close them," Phillip shouted.

"What?" I asked.

"Your eyes. Close them."

"How can I see her with my eyes closed, Phillip?" I said, thinking my best friend had forgotten how it worked.

"Bats back home don't have very good sight," He explained.

"Yeah, that's right, Whizzy," my sister interjected. "They use sonar waves to see everything."

"If LaCroiux is using his sorcery to hide her from our sight, we need to use our hearing to find her. That's why Vella knows where she is." Phillip sounded very confident.

Finally, I understood, "She can't see Grace, she can hear her movement."

"Exactly!" Phillip yelled with excitement.

I closed my eyes tightly and listened for her. At first I heard nothing except Phillip's webbed feet on the floor.

"Stand still!" I commanded.

The muffled voice became clearer. It started to become louder. I reached out my hands and began feeling around. My hands searched for anything. They landed against the wooden wall. I slid them around side-to-side and then up and down. Finally, I felt something that didn't feel like wood.

"Whizzy!" I heard Grace call in my head.

"I found her!" I yelled.

When I opened my eyes, she was sitting on the floor with her mouth covered in the clear paste I had seen earlier. She was also tied at the hands and feet.

I used my wand to free her. She leapt to her feet and hugged me so tightly I could barely breathe. I nearly passed out.

As I held her she felt small. When we let go I noticed her face...she looked so tired. Her usually light, gray-colored eyes were darkened, almost black. When she walked over to grab her sword and bow and arrow from against the wall, I realized just how tiny she had become. Her arms and legs looked weak and frail. Long white hair flowed around her face as she turned back toward me. She still looked beautiful.

We had finally found her. Vella had given us the information needed to find Grace. Now, we had to honor our bargain and release Goren.

Rachel approached Vella and Aevion. The young vampire bat touched her arm.

"Please, let me daddy go," He pleaded.

Rachel smiled at him and nodded. She reversed the spell, freeing Goren.

He fell to the floor. Aevion dashed to his father and hugged him. Goren was confused. It took him a moment to realize that his son had returned.

Grace Tallon wasted little time. She quickly challenged the rulers of The Deadly Spray Forest, Goren and Vella, to help us stop Sorcerer Pierre LaCroiux before he could reach the castle.

"You have an army at your command, Goren. Use them to help us stop LaCroiux before it is too late," She pleaded with him.

Aevion clung to his father's leg like a young child. His face still had the expression of fear. It made him almost look human, unlike his parents.

Goren seemed afraid to challenge the sorcerer. Vella, however, was fuming mad. "He must be stopped, Goren."

"Once he reaches the castle it will be nearly impossible to stop him. We must leave now. He will return, Goren. When he does, what will you do to stop him from taking over your home?" Grace sternly questioned the leader of the vampire bats.

Goren looked at how frightened his son was and realized that he couldn't allow Sorcerer LaCroiux to come back.

"We will help you."

"Now, how do we get out of here?" I asked.

Grace looked up. It was pitch black. She just pointed and said, "The sky."

Rachel grinned from ear to ear. She knew exactly what Grace wanted. Reaching her wand toward the darkness, she blasted a white-hot bolt of lightning skyward. It disappeared into nothingness. My heart sank. Phillip groaned. Rachel turned to look at Grace, but Grace just kept staring at the ceiling. Rachel returned her gaze skyward just as the bolt hit the roof and punched its way through. A loud explosion rocked the room. Light poured in, stinging my eyes. Strange sounds assaulted my ears, like rushing air and fast moving objects, followed by a series of thuds. I opened my eyes when Goren shrieked! A group of vampire bats had flown into the room when the roof blew off.

Goren then spoke to them, "Brothers! It is time to stop this sorcerer. We must help the elves of Cadieux. Now take to flight. We go to fight!" He yelled.

Each of us found ourselves flying through the open roof and into the sky upon the backs of the vampire bats. Grace and Goren were together at the lead.

Snow was still falling outside The Deadly Spray Forest, and we were off to Cadieux Castle.

BATTLE IN THE SKIES
16

Flying through the cold Mistasian air was amazing. It would have been better, but I had a pointy claw sticking me in the ribs. I could only imagine how badly Phillip's stomach felt right now. He was probably about to throw up.

"Whizzy! This is awesome!" He yelled at me.

I guess I was wrong. He had the biggest smile I had ever seen on a frog's face. It would have been from ear to ear, but frogs don't have ears...which I'm sure you already knew, so I'll move on.

The vampire bats followed in a strict formation behind Goren with three on each side. Vella flew in the middle behind Goren as she held Aevion tightly. Apparently, the little guy couldn't fly.

We quickly moved away from The Deadly Spray Forest, and now flew over a vast open land. There was nothing but white snow ahead of us.

"Where are we?" I shouted to Phillip.

"We are over the Mastodon Lands," Grace answered.

"Mastodons?" Phillip replied. "Like hairy elephants?"

Grace gave Phillip a peculiar look. She had no idea what an elephant was. "Efalant?" She questioned.

"No an el-a-fant!" Phillip tried to pronunciate.

"Phillip!" Rachel scolded. She just wanted him to stop talking. They could barely hear each other over the rushing wind. "Grace, are they dangerous?"

"Yes!"

"Great!" I muttered. Thankfully, they were on the ground, and we were in the air. That, however, wouldn't last long.

"Dragons!" Rachel warned.

Headed straight for us were five large scaly dragons. They ranged in color and shape. There was a red dragon with a large fan-like shield behind its head. Its tail was long and thin and pointed like a sword. A purple-colored beast flew next to it. That one was smaller in size but had spikes sticking out of its tail. Two golden dragons flew side by side. They had boils all over their skin and were very fat. The last dragon trailed behind the others. It was the largest of them all and dark green...like a lizard back home in Greenville. It looked the scariest, too. I could see its sharp fangs and forked tongue.

My first thought was which one breaths fire. I tried to remember which dragons could in Mistasia.

The vampire bats began shrieking, and the dragons screeched in response. It was awful.

"Grace!" I yelled over all the noise.

"What!"

"Which one breaths fire?" I screamed.

It was so loud I couldn't hear her answer.

"What?" I was now screaming like a scared little girl, as the dragons got closer. Gripping my wand tightly in my right paw, I aimed at the bright red dragon barreling down upon us. Before I could fire, Goren dove down, and we all followed.

A harsh rush of wind blasted my furry face. My eyes closed tightly. I could feel my cheeks being pushed against the wind and suddenly warmth surrounded me. Opening my eyes, I saw a dark reddish fireball was about to engulf me. I turned my head when the vampire bat released his grip.

I fell to the ground and landed in a fluffy pile of snow.

My body had sunk from the impact, but my legs, arms and head were all above the snow.

"My wand? Where's my wand?" It was gone. I had dropped it when I landed in the snow.

A loud thud startled me. Snow swirled around me, making it hard to see. When it cleared, the same bright red dragon I had been targeting earlier was creeping toward me.

It had blazing yellow eyes. I felt like they could see inside me. I searched for my wand as the dragon approached.

Finally, I spotted it near my right foot, but I was trapped in the snow, helpless. The dragon opened its mouth.

A shriek blasted in the air and a gray blur whizzed past me crashing into the dragon. Snow again whipped into the air. I could hear fighting.

I struggled to free my body. Twisting side to side, I wiggled my way free and grasped my wand as the dragon reappeared with a vampire bat riding him. I pointed my wand at them when they took to the air over my head, knocking me backwards into the snow again. Jumping to my feet, I searched the sky.

Above me, raged an amazing battle. The vampire bats and dragons danced about the sky like ballerinas on stage swirling in and around each other.

I heard footsteps in the snow.

"Whizzy, you're alive!" Rachel shouted as she wrapped her arms around me.

Grace and Phillip were right behind her.

"Whizzy, we must go," Grace commanded. "Goren will give us time to escape. These lands aren't safe with the dragons among us. There are few places to hide."

"Where do we go from here?" I questioned.

"Come this way." Grace grabbed my hand and ran. Phillip and Rachel followed as the sky above cried out with the sounds from angry beasts.

The purple dragon swooped down upon us. It was very low to the ground and gaining quickly. Its spiked tail stuck straight up like a hammer waiting to slam down on a nail. I really didn't want to be the nail.

Before it could attack Vella landed on its head and grabbed its horns. She twisted the dragon's head causing it to turn and crashed its wing into the snow. As the giant purple dragon tumbled through the snow, Vella leapt back into the air and rejoined the other vampire bats.

"That was way too close!" Phillip croaked.

Grace continued to drag me through the snow. She was so fast it took all the energy I had left to just keep from falling. Rachel and Phillip attempted to keep pace. I had no idea where Grace was going. Suddenly, she stopped. I slammed into her backside and tumbled into the snow, face first.

"Watch out, Whizzy." Grace mocked me.

Rachel and Phillip caught up. Phillip was breathing so hard I could hear him wheezing.

"Why... did...you stop?" Phillip said between deep breaths.

Grace spun around and glanced into the sky. "We don't have much time. Rachel, we need a place to hide!" She demanded.

"Like what?"

"Something that will cover us. Just do it quickly before the dragons see us. We need

something to create a visual shield." Grace
pressured.

"An igloo!" Phillip shouted. "Make an
igloo out of the snow."

Rachel smiled at him then held her
wand out and began to move it in the shape
of a circle. The snow swirled and created a
dome. The half circle wasn't very large, but
would be almost impossible to see from the
air. The igloo blended in to all the snow
surrounding us.

"Quickly! Get inside," Grace pushed
me.

"But it's so small," Phillip whimpered.

Rachel slid inside the small opening. I
followed. It was very small. The sunlight
from outside was faded through the thick
snow walls, but there was enough to allow
me to see Rachel jammed into the back
corner. I crawled over on my hands and
knees. Snow was stuck in my fur. It looked
like little balls of popcorn stuck all over my

body. I stopped for a second to try and turn around, but Grace started pushing me further into the igloo.

"Hey, cut it out, Grace!"

"Get in!" She barked at me.

It really made me mad when she yelled at me, but right now I couldn't do anything about it anyway. I was crammed between Rachel and the ice-cold snowy igloo wall. My legs were twisted like a pretzel and then Grace sat on them.

"Ouch!" I cried out.

"Get in here, Phillip!" Grace called in a panicked voice.

That was definitely not something I was used to from Grace. She was normally cool under pressure. This situation must have been far more dangerous than I even understood.

Phillip's green legs and froggy butt wiggled into the igloo. His webbed foot smacked me in the face. Grace and Rachel started to pull him in as he started to scream.

"I'm stuck. I'm stuck!"

The girls pulled and pulled, but Phillip's large green head was stuck in the entryway. The walls began to crack and snow began to fall into the igloo's entrance.

"Wait!" Rachel yelled to Grace. She pointed her wand at the entrance and it slowly began to widen.

Finally, it was large enough for Phillip's head to slide through. Once inside, the hole shrunk again.

I took the deepest breath I had ever taken in my life. This igloo wasn't going to provide much protection, if any of the dragons found it, but maybe we would get lucky and the vampire bats would be able to fight them off before that happened.

My eyes were so tired. I fought to stay awake as Grace and Rachel talked about escaping the Mastodon Lands. The last thing

I heard was Grace explaining how Sorcerer LaCroiux must have realized that we had escaped from The Deadly Spray Forest.

"The dragons have always worked with him. Sorcerer LaCroiux must know we have escaped."

THAT JUST MADE HIM ANGRY
17

"Whizzy!" a voice screamed in my head. It startled me awake. My eyes popped open so quickly that everything was hazy and unfocused, like looking in the bathroom mirror after a warm shower. I could hear a drum pounding in my head. It was my heart thumping. Shaking my head to try and wake up, I realized that Rachel and Phillip were looking out the small opening of our igloo.

"Close the opening, Rachel!" Grace demanded as she drew her sword.

I knew that wasn't a good sign. Jumping to my feet, I stumbled and Grace grabbed me.

"Wake up, Whizzy. We need to be alert." Grace was desperately trying to listen to something.

"What do you hear?" I whispered.

"Shh!"

Phillip and Rachel turned to see what Grace was doing. I remained as silent as I could.

We could all hear noises from outside the igloo, but nothing sounded familiar. Grace's elven ears, however, could make out much more than ours. She definitely was listening to something going on outside.

Phillip leaned against the cold snowy wall; placing his head to the wall, he concentrated to hear what was going on outside, too.

"Dragon?" Rachel mouthed.

Phillip didn't respond.

"Phillip, get away from there!" I screamed. Right about now, I was thinking that my best friend was an idiot, because if there was an angry monstrous dragon on the other side of that wall, he was going to get burnt to a crisp.

"I don't think it's a dragon?" Phillip responded. "Maybe it's a Mastodon?"

A deep inhaling sound echoed through the small opening in the igloo.

I looked at Grace hoping for a better explanation of what was going on outside than what Phillip thought.

"Get back!" She yelled at Phillip.

A horrid sound began outside like a jet's engines kicked into motion. The side of the igloo started melting. The snow darkened in color, and then a blast of red flames cut through the wall and shot across the igloo. It crashed into the wall next to me.

I let out a high-pitched squeal as the flame singed my tail. Jumping into Grace's arms, I fell onto the snow, taking Grace with me. I was lying on top of her when she pushed me off and gave me a dirty look.

A large hole had been burned into the side of our igloo. We had been found by the largest of the dragons that had attacked us...the scaly dark green beast.

One large, oblong orange eye peered into the igloo. A vicious roar shook its icy walls. Snow began to fall from the cracking ceiling.

Rachel ran toward me with her wand out. I thought she was going to zap me when the tip of her wand lit up bright white. I ducked to avoid her blast when she cast a spell against the wall behind me. The bolt exploded into the wall and shot a doorway for us to escape.

Rachel dashed through first, followed quickly by my best friend; both left me behind to face the angry dragon. Grace grabbed my arm and pulled me to my feet.

I flew into the air like a ragdoll as she yanked me outside.

The dragon spit fire again melting the igloo as we escaped.

Grace led our way through the snowy field. There was no place to hide and the dragon began to chase us. Luckily, he wasn't very quick. The beast's large paws made the ground tremble like an earthquake with each step. We had nowhere to go...nowhere to hide. It was obvious that we were going to have to stand and fight the dragon. That was when we stopped running.

Grace Tallon stood next to me with her sword at her side. She was breathing heavily. The wind blew her long white hair back from her face. Her cheeks were red from the cold and breath curled out from her pink lips.

Rachel stepped up on the other side of Grace, and Phillip stood beside me. The four of us now faced the slowly approaching enemy. A puff of smoke slithered out from the dragon's mouth. Its blood-red forked tongue ran across its top lip like someone that was about to eat dinner.

I didn't want to be anybody's dinner and especially this stupid dragon's. I was getting tired of things attacking us in Mistasia so I fired a spell to freeze the dragon. It was one of the few spells I felt worked well...but this time it didn't.

The dragon winced when my spell slapped it in the face. It angrily shook its head like attempting to rid itself of an annoying fly.

"Why did you do that?" Rachel snapped. "All you did was make it angry."

She was right...the spell hadn't worked and the dragon looked really angry.

"What now?" I replied.

Grace unexpectedly stowed her sword into its holster.

"What are you doing, Grace?" I pleaded for an answer. "Giving up isn't a great option. I don't want to be this guy's dinner!"

"Phillip, wait here. Rachel and Whizzy, get on either side," Grace commanded.

"What are you doing?" Rachel seemed worried.

"Phillip, be ready to jump," Grace added. Then, she sprinted away toward the dragon.

It roared and spit fire. Grace dodged the first blast by leaping to the right. The dragon attempted to hit her again, but she avoided that shot, too.

Rachel slapped my shoulder and began to run. I followed. While the dragon was distracted with Grace, my sister and I were able to position ourselves on each side of the giant lizard.

Phillip still stood looking confused in the same spot. He watched Grace in amazement as she danced around the dragon's attempts to burn her.

Grace jumped onto the dragon's shoulder and climbed onto its back. "Bury it!" She yelled.

Rachel and I began forcing snow up and over the dragon's body. It thrashed around kicking snow back at us with its thick massive tail.

A scorching fireball shot from the dragon directly at Phillip. I panicked as it flew toward my best friend in slow motion. I stopped what I was doing to watch in terror. This dragon wanted frog legs for dinner.

Phillip leapt straight up and over the fireball. He flipped in a somersault and landed on the dragon's back next to Grace.

That was awesome! I thought.

"Whizzy!" Grace yelled snapping me back to reality.

Rachel and I continued to force snow over the dragon's body, like waves crashing onto the beach.

The beast tried to turn its large head toward Rachel. She moved a wave of snow directly into its scaly face. When the snow hit the dragon, it stumbled to its knees. As the snow began to pile up, it began to struggle to stand. Suddenly, the giant beast roared again and pushed its massive wings skyward sending snow flying into the air. It looked like a blizzard.

Grace pulled her sword out and handed it to Phillip. She grabbed her bow and arrows. Phillip slashed at the dragon's right wing while Grace pierced its scaly skin with arrows.

The beast screamed in pain and began thrashing around in the snow again. Phillip was tossed off. He landed hard in the snow not far from me.

"Phillip!" I yelled.

He got up quickly and just ducked the dragon's whipping tail.

A swell of anger overtook me. I dug my feet into the snow and summoned all the strength I had to attack the dragon. I reached down and pushed my paws into the snow, then pulled up into the air like lifting a blanket. A huge pile of snow raised into the air creating a wall. The dragon disappeared behind it.

"Ahhhhh!" I yelled releasing all my anger and all the snow toward the dragon. It crashed in a powerful wave. When it settled, the dragon was gone, buried under nearly six feet of snow, but so were Grace and Rachel.

BURIED ALIVE

18

"Whizzy, what have you done?"
Phillip cried. He ran toward the hill of snow
where the dragon was buried. Phillip
shouted as he fell into a hole between the
new snow pile and us.

"Holy moly, this is a huge hole! Look
at this!" Phillip called from below. He stood
on brownish-green grass, something we
hadn't seen this whole time in Mistasia. I
had dug the hole when I used magic to toss
snow onto the dragon. This entire area had
shifted and now Grace, Rachel and the
dragon were underneath it on the other
side.

"Rachel." I became scared as I realized
she was missing. "Phillip!" I yelled to my
best friend.

We ran to the hill and began
searching for Rachel and Grace. Using my
paws, I dug through the snow. Phillip did
the same. It was taking too long. They
wouldn't be able to survive at this pace.

I held my wand out like a shovel and
began to dig. Each time I flicked my wand
snow flung off the pile. I frantically tossed
snow searching for them, even hitting Phillip
with some snow.

"Hey, Whizzy, watch out!" He croaked
at me.

"I have to find them, Phillip."

"Wait! Wait!" Phillip yelled. Then he
said nothing.

"What?" I growled back.

"Be quiet. I can hear Grace!" Phillip
was concentrating.

I was breathing very heavily. Each
breath exploded from my mouth like fire
from, ironically enough, a dragon.

Phillip walked around like a puppy searching for where it had buried a bone in the backyard. I slowly followed behind him in anticipation.

Just show me where do dig! I thought.

"There!" He pointed to a small pile near the top of the snowy hill.

The sun was setting and it was becoming very cold. We needed to find the girls and get to shelter quickly.

"Phillip, go find Rachel!" I pleaded and my best friend hopped off to where we last saw her.

I began shoveling again using magic. It wasn't long before I found Grace's leg. I stopped shoveling and began to dig her out by hand. She gasped for air when I freed her from the snow. After a few seconds she was completely free.

"Grace, are you okay?" I asked.

She punched me in the chest knocking me into the snow and then jumped on top of me.

"I should pound you, Whizzenmog!" She was furious. Just as she raised her fist, Phillip shouted.

"I found Rachel!"

Grace leapt off me and dashed to help. I quickly joined them.

The three of us eagerly dug her out of the snow. She wasn't breathing when Phillip pulled her free. He began to perform C.P.R. to revive her. Phillip placed his webbed hand under her neck and lifted slightly to open her airways. Then he moved in.

"What are you doing?" Grace sounded horrified. "This is no time for that!"

"What?" Phillip replied.

"No, it's okay," I told Grace.

The elven warrior gave me a confused expression as I motioned for Phillip to continue.

"He's trying to save her...not kiss her."
I explained to Grace who thought that my
best friend was trying to use this moment to
make the moves on my sister. "He is trying
to resuscitate her."

Phillip took a deep breath and then
placed his clammy frog lips over Rachel's
mouth and snout and exhaled. The first
attempt didn't work. Grace placed her hand
on my arm. I would have felt something, but
I was too numb with fear. Phillip tried again
and nothing.

"Rachel!" I muttered.

The sun had completely set now and
it was very dark. The moon didn't shed
much light tonight.

Tears started to form in my eyes. This
couldn't be happening. She couldn't be dead.

Phillip placed his hands over her chest
and began pushing down.

"One...two...three," He counted to
himself. Then he waited a second and did it

again. Phillip looked at me. All I could see was his bright red eyes in the darkness, but I knew he was crying, too.

"No!" was all I could say.

Grace looked at us not quite understanding what was happening. "Is she dead?"

"NO! Rachel you can't die!" I shouted. "Try again, Phillip!" I demanded. "Don't give up." I joined him by placing my paws over her chest. He did the breathing, and I pushed on her chest.

Phillip started to place his mouth over Rachel's again when she coughed and rolled to her side. She gasped for air.

"Rachel!" I yelled with excitement. I didn't even let her sit up before I hugged her. I had never hugged my sister so hard in my life.

DO YOU SEE WHAT I SEE?

19

Rachel had survived. I felt horribly...not that she had survived. I was grateful my sister was still alive, but that I had almost killed her and Grace because I wasn't able to control my anger. The powers I had in Mistasia made me dangerous to my own friends and family. I began to wonder if I should even stay with them.

It wasn't long after we saved Rachel from her snowy tomb that we began to move toward Cadieux Castle again.

"We cannot stay here," Grace said. "The night will provide us with cover to move. We have to go now. It is our best opportunity to try and reach Cadieux Village by morning."

Phillip carried Rachel in his arms. He held her so tightly. I could tell that he really cared for her. It had bothered me so much that he and Rachel were getting close after all these years. I felt like I was losing my best friend, but I'm really not. I'm gaining the sister I never had. Phillip had been able to bring Rachel and me closer. I should be thanking him.

His red eyes looked like two m&m candies floating in the air. I walked beside him, and Grace led the way. She seemed to be headed somewhere away from the castle.

"Grace, where are we going?" I questioned.

"Mastonia."

"Ah...excuse me. Mastonia?"

"The realm of the Mastodons, Whizzy." She replied with a laugh.

"I thought you said they were dangerous," Phillip questioned while he gazed at Rachel, who slept in his arms.

"Yes, they are to outsiders," Grace responded. "If you three entered Mastonia alone, they would be very angry. However, I will be with you."

She sounded very confident that these large hairy elephants wouldn't harm her.

"What does that mean?" I angrily snapped.

"Watch your temper, Whizzenmog. You don't want to bury us in snow again." She poked at me. "Besides the queen has protected these creatures. They will honor our treaty and help us. We can use them to travel to Cadieux Village tonight."

"Like ride them?" Phillip sounded uncomfortable with that idea. He probably imagined himself falling off and getting trampled.

"Yes, Phillip. We will need to ride one."

"One?" I was shocked. "They must be very large."

Grace never responded. She just gave me a sly smirk and kept walking. The moonlight led our way. To where I had no idea, but our guide most certainly knew where she was headed.

The moon had grown quite large in the wintry night sky. It had also become very bright. The Mistasian moon seemed to brighten as the nighttime moved along. We had been walking for what felt like an hour when Grace suddenly stopped. She placed her hand out behind her to stop us.

"Don't move," She whispered. She was watching something only she could see...which didn't make me feel any less uncomfortable about it.

"What do you see?" I asked because there wasn't anything in front of us but white fluffy snow...or so it appeared.

In the distance, was a large gorge hidden by the snow. From where we stood my eyes couldn't see the sliver of difference between the two sides of the gorge along the ground, but Grace could. We slowly crept up to it. She positioned herself down on her stomach and crawled to the gorge's edge. I followed.

When my head poked past allowing me to see into the gorge, I gasped. Grace slapped her hand over my fox mouth.

She shot me a disgusted look. "Be quiet, Whizzenmog. I don't need you blowing this. If you anger them, so help me, I will feed you to the dragons myself."

I couldn't believe what I saw below us. In the gorge was a huge city. Not like anything we had in Greenville or in Cadieux either. It was more like a jungle. There wasn't any snow, just bright green vines and trees and grass. Massive huts made from bark and tree limbs were lined up on one side. Then I saw one...a Mastodon. It was the biggest living thing I had ever seen, nearly the size of a cruise ship.

I turned around, "Phillip, you have got to see this!"

Grace grabbed my shoulder and pushed me into the snow. Her face appeared upside down over mine. "Maybe I didn't make myself clear...shut it!" She looked around for a way to get down into the gorge. "Stay here!" She commanded. Then Grace stood up, grabbed her bow and fired an arrow with a rope tied to the end. It flew through the air and slammed into the far side of the gorge. She pulled out her sword and stabbed the snowy ground before tying the loose end of the rope to its handle.

"I will be back soon." Then, she began to walk across the rope.

I watched in amazement. She never even stumbled on the thin rope. When she reached the other side, Grace jumped off onto a nearby rock and began to descend into the gorge. Quickly, she made her way down and finally disappeared behind the massive Mastodon huts.

"What if she doesn't come back, Phillip?" I asked.

"Grace will be fine, Whizzy. Don't worry."

"I'm not worried about her getting hurt...what if she leaves us here? We are helpless." Suddenly, I had the sinking feeling that someone was playing a practical joke on us, and we were going to be left stranded in a Mistasian snowstorm to die.

"She wouldn't do that. Would she?" Phillip suddenly didn't sound so sure either.

All I knew now was that the three of us were stuck up here in the cold, and Grace Tallon was below in the seemingly warm gorge attempting to get a Mastodon transport. Was this really happening?

MASTODON RIDERS

20

Rachel awoke just a few minutes after Grace had gone down into Mastonia. She was tired and confused, but still managed to be very mad at me. I should have expected that...I mean I did almost suffocate her under a mound of snow. That would have been difficult to explain to mom...where's my sister, you ask? Well, mom, she was being attacked by a giant fire-breathing dragon so I used my wizard powers to bury them both in snow. What's that? I'm grounded for life?

Well, maybe it wouldn't go exactly like that, but thankfully I don't have to explain any of this to our mom. She already thinks there is something wrong with me. Any stories about Mistasia and she'll put me on a funny farm.

I watched for any sign of Grace. It wasn't easy to see as the snow had begun to fall again. Somehow, the snow melted as it went below into the gorge. I could tell that the grass below was wet, so I knew that the snow must have been turning into rain as it hit the warmer air down below.

Right about now, I wished I had gone with Grace. Even with this thick fur, I was feeling the chill of winter in my bones. Rachel didn't look much better. Phillip was starting to turn a shade of bluish-green. We wouldn't last much longer.

A rumbling noise started, followed by trembling in the ground around us.

"Earthquake?" Phillip asked.

"I don't know," I replied.

"No, look!" Rachel pointed to a whitish-brown hairy Mastodon approaching us. Grace was perched on its back.

My mouth dropped open as my head tilted back to try and see her all the way up on top of the Mastodon. It was like she sat on top of a three-story building.

The Mastodon stopped and grunted. Then it lowered its trunk into the snow.

"Climb on," Grace urged.

Phillip helped Rachel up onto the beast's trunk and then joined her. The Mastodon lifted them up into the air and let go, tossing them down on its back. I could hear Phillip scream as he fell.

"Rachel! Phillip! Are you alright?" I shouted worried that they had been hurt. Then, I heard them laughing.

"We're fine, Whizzy!" Rachel replied with a huge grin on her furry fox face.

"Let's go, Whizzenmog!" Grace barked at me.

I tried to move...but I just couldn't. Instead I found myself staring at this gigantic furry elephant standing in front of me. Its leg was like a tree trunk, except where the leaves would have been was a sharp pointy tusk.

"What? You scared?" Grace teased me. She began to giggle...Rachel, too.

Phillip just looked at me. "Come on, Whizzy. It's cool. Don't be afraid." He spoke in my head so the girls wouldn't hear. I appreciated that he didn't add to my humiliation, but it didn't solve my worries.

"I'm not afraid," I lied. I was terrified. This creature was huge, and I hadn't had the best experiences with creatures in Mistasia this time around. **Do they remember the dragon? Or the eel-fish? I** thought.

I huffed over to the front of the Mastodon and waited for it to extend its trunk. Its two black eyes blinked at me. I wasn't about to be tossed around like a rag doll, so I took off at full speed, running up its trunk between its eyes and across its head, sliding to a stop in front of Grace.

"Nice," Phillip responded.

The girls stopped laughing. Grace smiled like she was actually impressed.

The Mastodon lifted its trunk into the air and trumpeted a tune, signaling our departure. We were off to Cadieux Castle on the back of a Mastodon. I hoped that this part of our adventure would end quickly and without anyone trying to eat or burn us.

The slow trip to Cadieux Castle was pretty boring. I know...everything up to this point had been exciting to say the least, but the last three hours had moved along like the Mastodon...painfully slow and uneventful. Don't get me wrong, that was fine with me. I would have been enjoying this part of our journey much more if it weren't snowing so hard that I felt like I was in one of those snow globes that sit on the mantle around the holidays with a snowman in them. You know the one's that you shake and snow flies all around inside, but your mom won't let you touch because you broke one when you were four years old, and she still doesn't trust that you can handle them?

Anyway, the snow made it very hard to see anything, so I hoped that this monster we were riding on knows where it's going.

Even worse was the horrible smell. This thing stunk so badly...I thought maybe Phillip had farted, but he never smelled this awful. I started to believe that the brownish color fur on the mastodon was actually poop stained. It was that bad!

Phillip agreed. Rachel wouldn't even talk about it. She just tried to ignore it, but I caught her holding her nose at one point, so I knew it was bothering her, too. Grace, however, seemed unaffected by it. Maybe she had no sense of smell. That had to be it because there was no way she could stand it otherwise. The smell was overpowering. It reminded me of when I am under the covers and I fart and then I move around and the covers fluff up. That sudden burst of horrid odor that hits me makes it hard to breathe. It was like that only it never ended.

I'd rather fight the fire-breathing dragon right now.

"How much longer?" I asked Grace with my nose plugged.

She shook her head in disgust. "You are so childish."

A gust of wind blew by, swirling the snow into a frenzy. The Mastodon stood still as the snow danced around us. It only lasted for a few moments, and when it stopped, the nighttime sky cleared.

The snow had stopped. Cadieux Castle was straight ahead in the distance. Lights from the village lit the way like an airport landing strip. It wouldn't be much longer until we reached the castle and faced Sorcerer LaCroiux once again.

THE EMPTY BEDROOM
21

We ran through the village to Grace's
house. Inside we dashed down the hallway to
the secret passage that we had used to enter
the castle on our last visit. Grace grabbed a
torch and led the way through the same
tunnel into the castle where we entered
through the door in the floor just like before.

I couldn't believe that we were here
again. It felt like we had just been in this
room, the princess's old bedroom, a few
months ago, but it looked like it hadn't been
slept in years.

"Thirteen years!" Grace reminded me.
She must have been reading my mind.

It looked exactly the same. The bed
and dressers were in the same place.

"The queen doesn't live here
anymore?" Phillip questioned as he wiped his
finger across the top of a dusty cabinet. He
held it up for me to see that his green finger
was now discolored from the dirt.

"She lives in another part of the
castle," Grace responded.

"Why doesn't the queen let you live
here? It is a lot bigger than your house?" I
replied without thinking. Grace had told us
last time that elves didn't live in large
homes. They preferred the outdoors.

"This room is for the future children
of the queen," she answered. After an
awkward silence she added, "I like my
house."

"I know," I responded. I felt like an
idiot. Sometimes I wished that I would just
think before I said things.

"We need to find Queen Merran,"
Grace announced as she opened the door.

Without warning, a flash of light exploded into the dark room. I could hear screaming and then the sounds of something hitting the floor.

Boom! Boom! Boom! It echoed against the stone walls.

I tried to yell for Grace, but nothing came out. The light was so bright that my eyes burned. I felt a zap against my chest. It began to hurt. It felt like my heart was beating a million times a second. The light began to fade. My legs started to tremble and I stumbled to my knees. I couldn't breathe. Gasping for air, I grabbed my throat.

Am I dying? I thought.

I fell to the floor. The sound of footsteps echoed in my ears. Two feet stopped next to me. I rolled over to see who it was. Sorcerer LaCroiux stood over me with an evil grin and then everything went black.

LACROIUX'S MASTER PLAN
22

"LaCroiux!" I yelled after gasping for air. Warmth surged through my body. I jolted to my feet and pointed my wand at a shadowy figure in front of me.

"Whizzy! It's me!" My sister cried out. She had awakened the others and me with a spell.

"What happened?" I asked her.

"I don't know. When Grace opened the door and the light burst in, I just used a spell to shield myself. Whatever came in slammed me against the wall. I must have hit my head. When I woke up, you were all knocked out on the floor. I tried to wake you up...that was when I realized that it must have been LaCroiux. His dark magic was

173

keeping you all from waking up," Rachel explained.

"He's already here?" Grace sounded uncomfortable.

"It must have been him. Who else could have done this?" Rachel questioned.

"The queen!" Grace dashed from the room and down the hallway.

We all followed her toward the queen's new chambers. Grace slid to a stop. The hallway we were in split.

"What's wrong?" I asked Grace while trying to catch my breath. "You don't remember which way?"

"Why did he come here?" Grace demanded.

"What? What do you mean? LaCroiux...are you asking what he came for?" I didn't understand why she wasn't running to the queen. She was the queen's protector. "What are you waiting for?" I asked.

"Which way, Grace?" Rachel interrupted.

"Phillip!" Grace yelled, startling my best friend.

"Yes!"

"I need you and Rachel to protect the queen!" She commanded.

"But...okay!" Phillip seemed unsure as to Grace's plan. "But where are you going?"

"Whizzy and I are going to find LaCroiux."

She directed Phillip to the queen's quarters down the hallway to our left. Grace grabbed a wooden stool that sat in the hallway and flipped it upside down.

"Get on!" She yelled.

I jumped in between the stool's legs.

"Grab hold and don't let go," she smiled as she tied a rope to the stool and then her belt.

Grace took off down the hallway in the opposite direction from where Rachel and Phillip had gone. We sped down the halls and around corners until she cut one corner too closely. The stool swung out and smashed into the wall. Two legs broke free. I grabbed hold of the front stool legs and Grace dragged me along the ground. We finally reached our destination and the wooden stool slid to a stop.

My hands hurt from gripping so hard.

"I never want to do that again!" I told Grace, who smiled. I think she enjoyed seeing me suffer. "Where are we, Grace?" I asked as I struggled to stand. My knees had stone burns...if that is even possible.

"This is where Cragon Cadieux is held. LaCroiux is here."

"How do you know?"

"I can feel his presence," Grace answered.

"If you can feel him, how did you not know he was outside the door earlier?"

Grace didn't answer immediately. She seemed ashamed. "I let my focus leave me. You asked me about my home. It bothered me...and I couldn't concentrate."

I didn't really know what to say to that. After a moment, the silence made me uncomfortable, so I blurted out the first nice thing I could think of.

"You have a nice smile." Sometimes I wish I couldn't talk. It would probably make things easier.

Grace shook her head like most girls at Greenville High School. Her expression was a cross between frightened and ashamed. Then she looked me in the eyes and began to laugh.

"You are something else, Whizzy."

I smiled back. I think that was actually a compliment.

"So what do we do, Grace?" I asked redirecting our attention to the fact that we now stood outside the door where the former evil king, Cragon Cadieux, had been held for more than a decade.

She pulled out her sword. It sparkled against the flame of a torch on the wall. "We go inside."

Grace reached for the handle, and the hairs on the back of my neck stood up. Time seemed to move in slow motion as I saw a spark leap from the metal handle and jump into Grace's skin.

I tried to stop her but wasn't quick enough. When I reached for her wrist to stop her, the spark zapped her. Grace flew backward into the stone wall opposite the door. Her eyes were still wide open and she lay on the floor twitching.

"Grace!" I yelled in a panic as I rushed to her side.

She was still breathing, but she couldn't talk. Her mouth moved, but there was no sound. I began to feel that violent building of aggression in the pit of my stomach. It swept through my body like a forest fire in the heat of the summer. My brows sunk around my eyes and I gritted my sharp fox teeth.

I snapped up straight, pointed my wand at the door and fired. A blue flame shot like a missile from a jet fighter across the hallway and exploded into the door. Shards of wood shattered across the floor and the door creaked open before falling from its hinges and crashing to the floor. Quickly, I moved through the opening with my wand at the ready.

"LaCroiux!" I growled. It was impossible to see anything in the windowless room. The tip of my wand began to glow as I thought about light. Being a wizard definitely had its advantages; being able to create light whenever I needed it was just one of them.

The room seemed empty as I scanned it with the stream of light produced by my wand's tip. Sounds of dripping water and the scrapping of sharp nails on the stone floor echoed inside. A large brown rat appeared in my light. Its movement startled me. That just made me angrier.

"Dumb rat!" I muttered.

"You're too late, Whizzenmog!" A strong voice boomed.

"Show yourself, sorcerer!" I demanded as I whipped my wand around trying to find where LaCroiux was hiding. "You can't hide forever, you coward!"

A sinister laugh began to grow. It became louder with each second. The voice echoed against the walls making it nearly impossible to figure out where it was coming from.

"Don't move!" LaCroiux barked as a bright circular object, looking like a hula-hoop my sister played with back home, came flying toward me.

I tried to dodge it but the hula-hoop just followed. It wrapped around me and tightened until my arms were pinned to my sides.

"I want you to watch me overturn everything you have worked to create." Cried Sorcerer Pierre LaCrouix.

A flame burst in the corner to my right and then another to my left. Now fires blazed all around me, brightly lighting the room. Standing before me was LaCroiux. He knelt down beside a black object with no particular shape. It didn't look like much of anything.

I struggled to free myself, but with every movement the hula-hoop-like lasso tightened more. My arms began to hurt and my hands tingled like they had fallen asleep.

"Whizzenmog, do you recognize this man?"

I didn't reply. I knew exactly who it was...Cragon Cadieux, Queen Merran's evil uncle who had ruled Mistasia before my sister, Phillip and I had overthrown him during our last trip to Mistasia.

"You probably don't see it do you? It's the face of the rightful ruler of Mistasia." LaCroiux said with anticipation in his voice. A flame appeared in his left hand. It danced like a belly dancer in the palm of his hand. Then, he slowly waved his hand across the stone black objects frame to reveal Cragon Cadiuex's monstrous expression. The expression he had when Rachel and I had frozen him solid during our battle. All the rage he had at that exact moment was still there staring at me through his icy tomb.

"Don't do it, LaCroiux! Did you forget he banished you?" I attempted to reason with the sorcerer.

He started to laugh as though I was telling him a funny joke. "Boy, that was long ago. He will forgive me once I've saved him from this icy prison and helped him to reclaim his throne!" He empathically replied.

The flame in his hand began to grow as he placed it against Cragon's face.

"NO, DON'T!" I screamed. When I started to move again, the binds around me tightened once more. The pain shot up my back and I fell to the floor. "Don't do this. You are making a mistake!"

I watched as the flame engulfed Cragon's body. The ice melted away quickly, and the former king's figure emerged. He collapsed to the floor.

"My Lord?" LaCroiux said as he pulled Cragon Cadieux's limp body from the puddle on the floor. "You are free."

The moment LaCroiux uttered the word 'free' Cragon's face came to life. The same evil smile he had ruled with returned.

"Ahhhhhh!" Cragon screamed releasing thirteen years of frustration. The force of his voice shook the room.

It also freed me from the sorcery that LaCroiux had been using to hold me captive. I wasted no time as I jumped to my feet and dashed out of the room. When I returned to the hallway...Grace was gone!

THE RUNNING FIRE
23

"Grace!" I yelled as a rumbling noise came from behind me. I turned around to see a fireball steaming toward me like a train. I jumped away at the last second. The fireball scorched the stone wall where Grace had been when I entered the room.

I ran as fast as I could yelling for Grace the entire time. **Where did she go? What happened to her?** I thought.

Another rumbling came up the hallway behind me. I was terrified to look back. When I did, I saw a strange fiery creature with no eyes charging at me. It was gaining on me. Its roar sounded like nothing I had ever heard before; the closest thing I could imagine was a cross between fingernails on a chalkboard and a crackling fire. The heat burned my feet, which made me run faster yet. I could barely breathe. My fur was wet and heavy. I wasn't going to make it.

Up ahead was the place where we had left Rachel and Phillip earlier. **Here was my only chance.** I thought. I mustered all the speed I could and dashed for the corner. At the last moment, I dove down the hallway to my left. The fiery creature went past bellowing in rage.

I slid along the stone floor until I slammed into the wall. It hurt badly, but at this point I would gladly settle for a few scrapes and bruises, if I could avoid being burned alive. I got up and walked back into the hallway again. Waiting for me just twenty feet away was the fiery creature. It snorted like a bull ready to charge a matador.

I whimpered like a two year old that had to go to bed early. I was sweating so badly now that I looked as though I had just gotten out of a swimming pool. Sweat dripped from my snout. Suddenly, I remembered my wand. I had been holding it the entire time. I was so frightened that I forgot I was a wizard.

"Hey, Red, did you know it is winter?" I said with a smile on my face.

The creature roared, shaking the walls so violently that dirt and pebbles fell onto my head from the ceiling.

I pointed my wand directly at where I thought its head was and fired. Nothing happened. I panicked and attempted a freezing spell again.

"Oh crap!" I gulped. The heat from this nasty beast was making it so I couldn't use my favorite spell...the one spell I had relied on most.

The fiery red monster shifted and two tentacle arms shot out from its side. They swung around like whips before the monster lashed out at me.

I ducked to avoid its first attempt, but the second landed on my tail. I screamed in pain and jumped into the air. Without thinking I swung my wand like a sword at the tentacle on my tail cutting it in half. The red monster cried out in pain. Now, we were even. I was shocked. I held my wand up and noticed a thin ray of light sticking straight out of the end creating a sword.

"Now, it's on," I yelled while running toward it crazily swinging my new weapon. This wand was awesome. I sliced LaCroiux's creature into a dozen pieces and then used my favorite spell to freeze all those little pieces before they could reform. The hallway now resembled a miniature mountain range.

I was impressed with myself. "That was pretty awesome," I announced. That was when I remembered that I was alone and no one had witnessed me defeating this fiery monster. "Great, now nobody's gonna believe me when I tell this story!"

Wandering the hallways of Cadieux Castle, I struggled to find Queen Merran's chamber. I also had no way to contact Phillip or Rachel, and my guide was missing. Walking through a hallway that looked identical to every other one in this castle, I noticed a pair of eyes on the ceiling.

"Don't move!" I pointed my wand at it. My heart was pounding. **What has Sorcerer LaCroiux sent now?** I thought.

"No, Whizzy! It is Aevion!" He pleaded.

"Aevion? How did you get here?" I was quite happy to see him. "Where are your parents?"

"They came looking for the sorcerer."
"Did they find him?" I asked.

Aevion didn't look happy. He began to cry. "He has them under his control again."

"Where are they now!" I commanded. I wasn't about to let him lose his parents again. "Follow me," he said.

Running through the hallways of Cadieux Castle had become somewhat of a new sport for me. It was so easy to get lost. Everything looked the same, but something was leading me somewhere. I wasn't sure where, but I knew that I had to get there...and fast.

Aevion tried to keep pace. He was flapping his wings and suddenly leapt toward the ceiling in an effort to catch up.

"Come on, Aevion. We will find your parents. I promise," I wasn't so certain but didn't want to worry him. He almost felt like a little brother. It was really strange. I instantly pictured him dressed up in my clothes playing in my basement back in

Greenville. It made me smile. That would be a very weird conversation with my mom.

We approached a dead end, and I skidded to a stop. Aevion wasn't so slick. He slammed into my back and we fell to the hard stone floor.

"Ouch," I cried as I felt my knee throbbing. Blood trickled down my leg. The dark red blood mixed with the orange color of my fur. I wobbled when I stood up. A sharp pain shot up my leg.

"Where do we go now?" Aevion questioned as he stared at the stone walls before us.

"Why would this hallway end?" It made no sense to me. This hallway had come a long way to suddenly end. "There must be a hidden door," I mumbled. "Just like in Grace's home," I said to myself thinking about the trap door that lead us from her home into the castle.

"What?" Aevion replied.

191

"Whizzy, use your wand," Grace's voice echoed in my head.

A smile suddenly spread across my face. I pointed my wand at the stone wall and fired. A bright white bolt burst from the tip of my wand.

Aevion gasped.

The wall exploded and dust and light filled the air.

Aevion coughed and covered his face with his bat wings. I ducked my snout into my furry arm. When the dust cleared, another brightly lit hallway appeared, but this one was far different than any other in Cadieux Castle.

HIDDEN HALLWAY

24

"What in the world?" I gasped. I couldn't believe my eyes. It was like a totally different world behind this stone wall.

Bright light streamed through the broken stone wall. The walls were covered with brilliant green vines and colorful flowers. Warmth swirled around my body, like standing too close to a fireplace. There was no snow; I couldn't believe my eyes.

Aevion began to whimper and then screech.

"What's wrong, Aevion?"

"The light hurts!" He cried.

I felt a tingling in my paws, and injured knee; it's like that slight pain I feel when my feet are cold and I place them into warm water. It stings, but then I am just fine a few minutes later.

My vampire bat friend, however, didn't look well. His grayish-colored skin was glowing. Well, actually Aevion was transparent...I could see every bone in his body. I could even see his heart racing in his chest.

"Back away from the light, Aevion!" I yelled.

The young vampire bat's skin returned to its normal hue.

"I'll have to go alone."

Aevion looked scared.

"Your parents may be in there. I have to go. You will be fine. Just hide like you did before." I pointed to the ceiling and watched as he climbed up into the shadows until only his eyes remained. "I'll be back soon." Then, I took off running.

This new hallway seemed to go on forever. I stopped to catch my breath. My heart was pounding so hard, and I struggled to breath. The air was so hot it felt like I was breathing sand through my lungs. My throat began to close. I started to panic.

Laughter echoed through the air. It was Cragon Cadieux.

I couldn't see him. I tried to shout, but my throat hurt. Nothing came out.

"Having trouble are we, Whizzenfox?" Cragon's voice boomed before he appeared through the bright light. As he walked toward me, everything behind him died. The trees collapsed, vines shriveled and light disappeared. It was as if he sucked the life from every living thing around him. He slowly walked past me. Vines shot up from, the now, dirt-covered floor and tangled themselves around me. Cragon circled me like a lion ready to pounce on its prey. Almost all the light from the hallway was gone. It was now gloomy and dismal like the rest of the castle. The walls were moss covered and it stunk like the boy's locker room at Greenville High School.

"Well, Whizzenmog...it appears that you definitely aren't the brains of your family. Like a moth to the flame...you were simple prey." Cragon Cadieux stared at me. His beard had gray hairs sticking out. His eyes were cold and harsh.

"You deserved what you got, Cragon!" I yelled while struggling to free myself from the vines tangled around my wrists.

"Deserved?" He yelled so loudly it shook the room. Cragon leaned in close and whispered into my ear. "Then let's see what you deserve!"

He slowly backed away from me. I didn't move...I was stunned. What could he mean? What would he do?

I saw motion in the darkness behind Cragon. Out from the shadows came

Sorcerer LaCroiux and Grace. She was bound with her arms behind her back.

"Grace!" I yelled.

"Don't do anything he says, Whizzy!" She said to me in my head to avoid Cragon or LaCroiux overhearing.

"Grace Tallon. Protector of the queen," Cragon spoke with sarcasm. "Oh...where is the queen? Have you lost her?" Cragon and LaCroiux began to laugh.

"Whizzenmog...have you ever heard the phrase 'eye for an eye'?" Cragon asked. He had a smug look on his ugly face.

I didn't respond.

"That's right; how silly of me...you're not the smart one. I'll explain."

The sound of his voice made me very angry, but the more I struggled to free myself the tighter the vines twisted around my wrist.

"You remember when you and your sister cast a spell on me...freezing me? Now, you get to watch me do it to her." Cragon pointed his finger at Grace. Then, he opened his hand. A blast of icy mist shot from the palm of his hand and covered Grace.

"NO!" I yelled, but it was too late. She was now frozen solid, just like Cragon had been just an hour ago.

"Eye for an eye!" Cragon walked up to me again and whispered into my ear. "Your sister is next."

A jolt of rage fired through my entire body, "NO! Cragon I will stop you!" I screamed.

Cragon grabbed me by the neck and squeezed. He looked very angry. "Don't waste your breath, Whizzenmog. You can't stop me this time. Soon enough you will join them all. I will save you for last, and then when I'm finished...I'm going to place you all around my castle as statues to commemorate my great victory and reclaim my throne."

"Not...if...I...have...anything...to...say...ab out...it," I struggle to speak as he held my throat.

Cragon released his grip on me and took a step back. A wicked smile brushed across his bearded face. Then, he walked back into the darkness and disappeared into the shadows.

ALONE WITH A STATUE
25

This trip to Mistasia was beginning to feel more like a horrible nightmare. I just couldn't escape. I found myself hoping that when I reopened my eyes I'd find myself laying on the couch in the basement of my parents' house back in Greenville. I would give almost anything to be relaxing there right now...not caring about anything else, just watching some stupid TV show and trying to not fall asleep early.

Unfortunately, I wasn't there. "Grace?" I muttered when I reopened my eyes. The only thing I could see in the room was her figure staring at me helplessly. Her eyes looked like a scared child that had lost her parent.

A tear rolled down my furry cheek. I found myself crying alone with a frozen statue, which just happened to be a friend of mine.

I struggled to free myself from the vines that tangled around my wrists. I was helpless. My wand lay on the ground between Grace and me, but there was no way for me to reach it.

Tears streamed down my face. I hadn't cried since I'd lost my favorite toy when I was five years old.

Grace made me feel something that I had never felt before. I needed to help her.

Sorcerer LaCroiux reappeared from the shadows. He slowly walked by Grace and placed his hand on her head. He tapped his fingers on her like on a tabletop. Then, he turned and looked at her face.

"Uh," He said in disgust. "Not a good look for an elf."

"Shut up. LaCroiux!" I barked.

He just smiled. It was obvious that he was trying to make me angry.

"Where are your friends, Whizzenmog? You should be saving this girl! Hurry; don't wait!" LaCroiux mocked my situation. He laughed heartily.

I couldn't do anything to save her. Phillip and Rachel were nowhere to be found, and I couldn't reach my wand.

"Sorry, Whizzenmog, it's too late." Sorcerer LaCroiux smiled and swirled his hands over Grace Tallon's frozen figure. A whirl of wind and light entered the room and funneled around her like a tornado. A flash of light exploded into the dark room. Then, they were both gone.

A LITTLE TOO LATE
26

I screamed at the top of my lungs. My frustration made it hard to think. LaCroiux knew my weakness...it was me. I had always been my own worst enemy. Right now, I had to figure out how to escape, find Phillip and Rachel, and save Grace.

"Whizzy!" I heard a familiar voice cry out. It was my best friend, Phillip. Following behind him was Queen Merran, my sister and our new vampire bat friend, Aevion.

Rachel freed me using her wand. I fell to the floor. My body hurt badly. It felt like I had just lost a boxing match. Phillip helped me back up.

"Whizzy, where have you been? Rachel and I have been looking for you everywhere!" Phillip excitedly explained. His skinny arms wrapped around me while hugging me so tightly I nearly couldn't breathe...which was now the second time that had happened in this room.

"Where is Grace, Whizzy?" Rachel questioned.

I couldn't answer. How would I tell them she was gone?

"Gone?" Phillip said as he released his grip on me.

I just looked at him. There weren't any words left. My heart sank when I saw the image of her face in my head. I knew that Phillip would see it too.

My best friend gasped. "No! How did it happen?"

"Cragon!" Queen Merran empathetically responded.

Our journey had been so crazy I hadn't realized that this was the first time I had seen Queen Merran since we arrived back in Mistasia. She hadn't changed at all, despite the thirteen years that had passed since our last visit. Her rosy cheeks kept her youthful appearance. The only different was her hair was tied on top of her head beneath her crown.

I shook my head as another tear rolled down my cheek. I was too distraught to speak to the queen.

"Cragon's free?" Rachel yelled as she grabbed my arm and spun me around to face her. "Whizzy, talk to me! What is going on?" She was frantic.

I explained to them how Sorcerer LaCroiux had released Cragon Cadieux, captured me and turned Grace into a frozen statue.

"He plans to reclaim the throne," Queen Merran calmly spoke.

"They were too strong. I couldn't stop them alone."

"We were too late!" Rachel said. She looked so sad.

Phillip was in shock. He seemed to be waiting for someone to tell him what to do.

"We need to find Grace. She must be somewhere around the castle." I began to run back through the hallway. It looked vastly different than when I first entered. Slimy, brown vines clung to the walls that were stained and gross. The floor crackled underneath my paws from the dried leaves and vines. The smell was awful, like rotten potatoes.

"What makes you think they would put her outside?" Rachel questioned my sanity more than the actual fact that Grace would possibly be outside. "Anyone could see her."

"That's why. Cragon plans to reclaim the throne. So taking the queen's bodyguard prisoner and placing her exactly where everyone in Cadieux Village would see her would frighten them all. No one will challenge him then."

I lead them through the halls back to where I had fought with the fiery beast earlier. Up ahead was a corner. I slid to a stop. The others did, too.

"What is it, Whizzy?" Phillip whispered in my head.

I placed my finger over my mouth to tell everyone to be quiet. Rustling noises came from around the corner. It sounded like knives scrapping along the stone floor.

I gripped my wand tightly. My heart pounded. Right now, I hoped it wasn't LaCroiux. Two elongated shadows appeared on the floor. Reaching back, I used my arm to block my sister from being noticed.

"What is that?" Phillip again spoke to me using his telepathy.

"I don't know."

CRAGON TO GREENVILLE
27

The figures jutted out from around the corner like two mountaintops peaking against the setting sun as they blocked the light from the torches on the wall.

Aevion whimpered as Queen Merran Cadieux held him closely while standing behind Phillip. He curled up into a small ball under her arm.

Rachel and I caught eyes. She and I had been at odds for almost all our lives...now we stood together ready to fight whatever was about to attack us. It was funny how things had changed in our lives over the past six months. Mistasia had given me one very important thing...the sister that I had always wanted. A smile spread across my face.

Rachel seemed surprised by my sudden state of joy. I could tell she believed that I had just gone completely insane at that exact moment. I winked and turned back to face our oncoming foe.

The figures came around the corner. They were very thin and tall. Rachel and I jumped to our feet and pointed our wands at them. When the tips of our wands lit up to fire, we realized that it was Vella and Goren who stood before us.

"Mom!" Aevion screamed.

"Goren. Vella. Where have you been? Aevion said that you were captured by LaCroiux," I was surprised to see them walking the hallways...alone. "Who is with you?"

"We are alone, Whizzenmog," Goren replied. "We escaped from the sorcerer."

"Great. We could use your help," I began when Goren interrupted me.

"You all must leave this castle immediately."

"But...what?" I said completely confused. "We have to find Grace."

"I will send my friends to find her, Whizzenmog. You must come with us now." Goren was determined to get us away from Cadieux Castle, which was concerning me until he finally explained.

"Goren, we can't leave yet. Cragon escaped and this castle is under attack!"

"I know. He is in Wolverine Forest."

Phillip and I shared a concerned glance.

"Where is he going?" Rachel anxiously asked.

"He is headed from where you came."

"Greenville?" We questioned together. Goren nodded.

"How do we get out of this castle?" I demanded.

Queen Merran led our group to a hidden doorway near her quarters. It led us down a set of narrow hallways. They were extremely dark and wet. Queen Merran came upon a wall. She searched along the dirt-covered wall for a way to release the door. When she grabbed hold of a thick tree root she pulled down and the wall lifted upwards.

A rush of crisp cold winter air flooded the hall. It slammed against my body and sent a chill up my back. My fur rustled against the air.

We all escaped out into the village. We were in an unfamiliar area at the base of the castle. A small path allowed us to wander back into nearby Cadieux Castle. There, we encountered something no one expected.

The crowds in the village were panicked. They were all running and screaming. When we entered an opening in the square in the middle of Cadieux Village, we instantly noticed why.

Cragon's war had begun. A group of trolls were running amok. Rachel dashed off to save a little elven girl. She grabbed the girl just before the troll's large foot slammed down into the snow.

Phillip rubbed snow on his legs. The friction heated the snow making it melt. The water quickly absorbed into his amphibian skin. It gave him unbelievable strength. Phillip the Frog leapt into action. He hopped onto the head of one troll. A second troll noticed him and swung its massive club-like hand punching the other troll directly in the face. Phillip jumped away just in time. The troll tumbled and fell onto a house crashing through the roof and hitting the fireplace. Flames quickly spread through the small house, which now was ablaze.

"Phillip! Watch out!" I yelled as the troll closed in on him.

The troll slammed its fist like a hammer. Phillip leapt away again, but the force of the troll's punch was like an earthquake. It shook the frozen snow-covered dirt causing a massive crack in the ground that sped directly for me.

I didn't move quickly enough and fell into the small crack up to my waist.

Goren reached down and snatched me up by the scruff of my neck. He sped across the snow and grabbed Queen Merran. Suddenly, more vampire bats appeared in the sky. They swooped down and attacked the trolls in Cadieux Village. One grabbed Rachel. Another snatched Phillip by his webbed feet.

We were soaring through the sky and moving back toward Wolverine Forest. With the battle behind us now, I could see fires raging in the village against the white wintry background.

Phillip hung upside down next to me. "We have to go back!" he yelled at me.

"Goren, we have to help them!" I pleaded.

The vampire bat leader calmly responded, "You are needed elsewhere. Cragon must be stopped."

Suddenly, I remembered what Goren had told us earlier. Cragon was headed to Greenville, and we definitely had to stop him before he traveled to our world.

My mind raced as we flew toward our destination. I hoped that Cragon was alone. Rachel, Phillip and I had to figure out how to stop him before he entered the portal to Greenville.

EYES IN THE TREES
28

My paws landed so hard on the ground that it sent a sharp pain into my neck and back. Stumbling, I struggled to keep my balance when Goren grabbed hold of me.

"Thanks," I said.

We stood at the edge of Wolverine Forest, the same place where we had begun our journey nearly seven days ago. We had unfinished business here in Mistasia. I had no intention of leaving tonight.

Rachel walked beside me, with Phillip directly behind me. The vampire bats had gathered around Goren and Vella, but Aevion, who had traveled here with his mother, was now standing with the queen.

"Cragon?" I called. "Show yourself, you coward."

"Those are brave words for a child," the former king answered. "You definitely have heart, Whizzenmog. However, that is why I have had a change of heart."

Rachel scoffed, "I doubt that."

"Where are you, Cragon?" I called out again. He was nowhere to be seen, and now neither were our travel companions. "Where's Goren?" I asked my sister.

"That can't be good," Phillip gulped.

"Mom!" Aevion screeched. The queen held him tightly once again.

"Something is very wrong, Rachel" I pointed out just as I saw two wicked blazing eyes hiding in Wolverine Forest. "Wolverines!" I cried out.

Cragon's voice boomed through the air, "No...something far worse." Then, he chuckled like a deranged clown. "I see you have brought the fair princess with you tonight, Michael Whizzenmog!"

"Queen!" Phillip croaked.

"Not anymore, Phillip Harper!"

Cragon Cadieux appeared from the darkness of Wolverine Forest. His dark figure silhouetted against the white snow.

"My crown please, niece!" Cragon reached out and the crown flew from her head and into his outstretched hand. As he walked toward us he placed the golden crown upon his black-haired head.

Rachel fired a spell at Cragon, who blocked it with ease. I tried my best to stop him too, but Cragon deflected my blast as well.

He began to chant in a deep voice. It was utterly frightening. The ground started shaking and the snow began to swirl around us. It was a blizzard within seconds.

I could barely see anyone else. Reaching out, I grabbed Phillip's arm. He did the same to Rachel. We had all grabbed a hold of each other in the white out.

Cragon's voice bellowed one last time over the rushing wind, "I return you to where you belong."

My feet lifted from the snow. I felt a violent tug on my body and suddenly everything was spinning like I was trapped in a washing machine.

Everyone screamed as we flew through the air. When it stopped, we found ourselves lying on the carpet in my parents' basement.

I sat up quickly as the sunlight shined through the sliding glass door, which had already changed back from the portal to Mistasia into the window to our backyard.

Cragon had won. He had managed to trick us and send us back from Mistasia. Now, he was left to rule Mistasia all alone.

RAINER WHIZZENMOG

29

My breathing was heavy and my heart was racing against my chest. I felt sick to my stomach, partly because of the roller coaster return from Mistasia but also because of how we had left things.

Searching around the basement to see how many had returned with me I quickly saw my best friend lying face first on the carpet. He was still passed out. Phillip didn't travel well, so he was probably going to throw up when he awoke. Rachel was next to him. That was when I noticed that they were holding hands. A brief smile came over my face, which was no longer furry. I must have been okay with it, because normally I would have felt the urge to punch Phillip in the head.

I struggled to stand up. I was so tired. My whole body hurt. I mean places that had never hurt before, like the inside of my feet and ears, were throbbing.

"Where is Aevion?" I muttered to myself. I couldn't remember what he would turn into in our world. **Was it a bat? Maybe a rat?** I thought to myself. I reached down and shook my sister to wake her up.

She gasped and shot up slamming her head into mine. "Agh, Whizzy!" She barked at me.

We both rubbed our head in pain. Now, I could add something else to the list of things that hurt on my body.

"Are you trying to scare me to death?" Rachel continued to verbally assault me.

"Rachel, Whizzy?" our mom called from at the top of the basement stairs. She sounded surprised to hear our voices.

My sister and I panicked. "What do we do?" It had been about seven hours since we had traveled to Mistasia and it must be early in the morning. Rachel and I...well mostly me, weren't morning people so it would definitely be weird that we were up...and dressed!

"You two are up mighty early! You do realize you're on winter vacation, don't you?" Our mom continued as she walked down the stairs; she was still in her pajamas and bathrobe.

Rachel and I gave each other a scared glance when she noticed Phillip sleeping on the floor.

"Michael? Why is Phillip sleeping on the floor?"

"Ah." I was not even sure how to answer. My mind searched for a response that would fit.

"Oh, you know...he is such a klutz that he fell off the couch," Rachel told our mom. She gave me a strange look and then elbowed me in the arm. "Right, Whizzy?"

Mom was giving me a questioning look, probably because Phillip was nowhere near the couch. **Thanks a lot, Rachel!** I sarcastically thought.

"Oh...yeah. He fell and he must have been having a dream and he was crawling away from a monster and then the monster attacked and he sprawled out on the floor to pretend he was dead so the monster would leave him alone and..." I was rambling out of nervousness. Rachel looked like she was going to slap me. Her eyes nearly popped out of her head. I nervously started laughing and said, "I mean...um...yeah, he fell."

My mom just shook her head. She had always thought I was weird, but this conversation wasn't changing that. "Okay, Michael. I'm gonna go have a cup of coffee. You kids come up for breakfast. Okay? Your grandfather will be coming later today, so I'll need your help cleaning up the house."

After my mom went back upstairs, Phillip finally woke up and he did get sick. It wasn't pretty.

"Phillip! You are cleaning that up, man," I barked.

"I know," he replied as he went upstairs to get cleaning supplies.

Meanwhile, Rachel and I searched the basement for Aevion and Queen Merran.

"What did Aevion change into again?" I asked my sister.

"A mouse!"

"Mouse! That's right."

"Mouse!?" Mom yelled from the top of the stairs.

"On the TV, Mom! We are watching cartoons," I shrugged my shoulders after Rachel gave me a strange look. "It was the first thing I thought of!"

"I found him," Rachel announced as Phillip reentered the basement.

"Now, we just have to find Queen Merran. What do you think a queen would become?" I asked.

"Cat!" Phillip answered.

"Really? I would think something cooler like a giraffe or a zebra." I jokingly responded.

"You're an idiot. Do you think a giraffe would be hard to find in this basement?" Rachel snarked.

"I was just kidding."

"No, guys, look. A cat," Phillip pointed at a pure white cat with a black-tipped tail and bright blue eyes standing at the sliding glass door.

"We don't have a cat," I said and then immediately wished I hadn't.

"You need to stop talking because you're gonna hurt yourself, Whizzy." Rachel looked tired, frustrated and ready to physically hurt me.

Phillip picked the cat up and held it to his face. "Queen Merran?"

"I'm afraid I am no longer queen, Phillip Harper."

Phillip's face frowned when he heard the now princess's voice sadly reply to his question.

"Well, we all made it here safely." Rachel summed up our current state. "Now how do we get back?"

We all looked at each other blankly.

"Aevion, you brought us to Mistasia before; you can do it again!" Rachel pleaded.

"I'm sorry Rachel Whizzenmog, but I do not have any more of the mushrooms that I used to open the portal." He replied with a sad tone.

"Hey, Princess...can you take us back? We don't know how to open the portal.

Someone always comes to get us." I said hoping she had an answer.

"I cannot open the portal to my home, Michael Whizzenmog, but there is someone in your world that can."

"Really?" Phillip replied.

"Who?" Rachel and I questioned in unison.

"Your grandfather, Rainer Whizzenmog," Princess Merran replied.

A GRAND GIFT

30

"I can't believe that we forgot," Rachel groaned as she punched me in the arm.

"Forgot what? Rachel, I don't understand," Phillip said as the crease between his eyes formed. It always appeared when he was trying to remember something he thought he knew.

"Our grandfather brought our family to Greenville," I instantly remembered.

"Yes. Rainer Whizzenmog created the portal between our worlds many years ago. He is the link. Your grandfather will be able to open the portal and send us back," Princess Merran explained.

"Mom said he is coming today!" Rachel excitedly announced.

"That is unbelievable," I said.

"Yes, that is a grand gift of fortune. Your grandfather was an extremely powerful wizard. He could help turn the tide in our favor," the princess said. "You must convince him to help us."

Princess Merran and Aevion remained hidden in the basement as Phillip, Rachel and I helped clean the house.

That afternoon my grandfather arrived. I couldn't wait to get him away from mom and talk to him about Mistasia. He would understand. Each hour that past in our world was another day that King Cragon Cadieux ruled in Mistasia. The longer he reigned the harder it would be to remove him.

I had always admired my grandfather. He was a strong man, with a salt and pepper beard and short white hair. I never really knew what he did for a living. Rachel and I had never asked, but we always imagined it was something cool and important, but never would we imagine that he was a wizard from another world.

After dinner, I was becoming much more anxious. Rachel and I nearly dragged him downstairs as Mom and Dad cleaned up the kitchen.

"Grandfather, we have something to show you in the basement," I pressed.

"What do you have for me, Whizzy?" He replied while sitting on the couch in our basement.

"Something amazing happened to us this past summer," I began to explain. "Rachel, my best friend Phillip, and I traveled to another world."

"Well, that sounds exciting," Grandfather giggled. "Tell me about it." He moved forward in his seat to listen.

"Where did you go, Whizzy? Don't keep it a secret, my boy." He chuckled again.

"Ah...well, we went to..." I stammered. **Just say it, Whizzy!** I yelled at myself. Suddenly, I was very nervous. I feared my mom finding out about Mistasia, thinking she would put me in the loony bin, so telling my grandfather seemed like breaking some family rule or something.

"We have been to Mistasia!" Rachel blurted out.

"What?" Our grandfather's expression harshly changed. "You've been where?"

"Mistasia," I softly replied. I was beginning to regret this conversation.

"No." His eyes searched us over as if he thought we were joking.

"We have been there twice, Sir," Phillip added.

"Yes, we were just there. We returned only this morning, Grandfather," Rachel excitedly burst out.

I was hoping for a much better reaction, but we definitely hadn't gotten one.

"Grandfather, are you okay?" I asked, as he remained silent for a while.

He slid back in the couch and took a deep breath before exhaling. A tear rolled down his left cheek and then a smirk hit his lip. When he turned to face us, he asked, "Wasn't it the most wonderfully beautiful place you've ever seen?"

"Yes," I answered.

"It's been so long that I have almost forgotten what it looks like." He fought back more tears.

"You could go there again," Princess Merran said from Phillip Harper's lap.

My grandfather's head turned so briskly I thought he had snapped his neck.

"Excuse me?" He laughed.

"This is Princess Merran Cadieux, Grandfather. She was queen until her uncle,

King Cragon, sent us back here. He has taken over Cadieux Castle," I explained.

"Yes, and we need your help to get back to Mistasia," Rachel added as she grabbed Grandfather's hand.

"How?"

"You must reopen the portal to Mistasia, Rainer Whizzenmog. It is time you return to your home and reclaim your proper place in our world," Princess Merran urged.

He sat silently for a moment; a glimmer in his eye began to shine and a smile gleamed across his face.

Then, he spoke, "Yes...I believe you're right."

SNEAK PEAK

LAST EMERALD

PHILLIP & WHIZZY TRILOGY (BOOK 3)

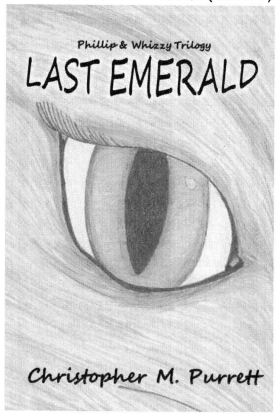

RACHEL WHIZZENMOG

1

My name is Rachel Whizzenmog, and I have an unbelievable story to tell you. It all began last summer when I was kidnapped by a snake and dragged off to another world called Mistasia. I know that's not what you were probably expecting to hear from a fifteen-year-old girl, but it's true.

Mistasia is a beautiful and dangerous world that I enter through the sliding glass door in my basement. My grandpa once lived in Mistasia long ago as the protector to the King.

In Mistasia, my twin brother, Michael, who we call "Whizzy", and his best friend, Phillip Harper, saved me from the evil King Cragon, who turned out to be a sorcerer.

That's not all...six months later, just before Christmas we all traveled back to

Mistasia. When we arrived, it was winter there too and awfully cold...oh, did I mention my brother and I turn into foxes and Phillip becomes a frog in Mistasia?

Phillip, Whizzy and I were brought back to Mistasia by a young vampire bat named, Aevion. The sorcerer, Pierre LaCroiux, was controlling his parents, Goren and Vella. They tricked us and helped King Cragon return to power.

Now, Phillip, Whizzy and I found ourselves trapped, but not in Mistasia...in our hometown of Greenville. We needed to get back and help Queen Merran reclaim her throne from her uncle, the king. It seemed almost hopeless until we realized we had a secret weapon coming over for Christmas holiday, our grandpa...Rainer Whizzenmog.

A LITTLE PRIVACY

2

I looked into the bathroom mirror.

I look awful. I thought to myself.

My eyes were red like I had been crying for days and my hair was a complete mess. Grabbing the nearest hairbrush from the drawer I started to tame my hair. Suddenly, I caught a frightening scent. My clothes were damp and smelled like Whizzy's sweaty gym socks. Yikes!

I need to take a shower before Phillip thinks I'm some wild animal. I told myself. That was probably the best idea I'd had in some time. I needed to relax and unwind. The tension in my neck was causing me to hunch over. I just kept thinking about the poor helpless creatures of Mistasia and the awful things that King Cragon was doing to punish them now that he was back in power. Princess Merran was correct...we needed to get back right away. Every hour we waited here in Greenville, another day passed in Mistasia. Cragon wouldn't wait very long to take his revenge.

The hot water from the shower felt great. It was definitely much better than the cold air in Mistasia. Stepping from the shower, I reached for my towel and quickly wrapped it around me.

I heard a creaking noise while I was drying my hair and quickly stopped. The door was slightly open.

"Whizzy!" I yelled, thinking my stupid brother had opened the door to let in a cool draft. He was always doing dumb things like that to make me mad. I made sure the towel was wrapped around me tightly and stuck my head out into the hallway to yell at him, but there was no one there.

I scoffed. Maybe I just hadn't closed the door tightly enough. This was a very old house and the doors would sometimes creak open. Whizzy used to think it was haunted when we were kids. Pushing against the door harder, I heard it click. Then, I locked it...just to be sure.

When I turned around, I screamed. Standing in the middle of the floor was a small black mouse.

"Aevion! I'm naked," I shouted angrily while pulling my towel close between my legs and crossing my knees.

The small black mouse was the same vampire bat that had taken us to Mistasia the day before. He had been sent back to Greenville with us when his parents, Goren and Vella, the leaders of the vampire bats, betrayed us. Sorcerer LaCroiux kept them under his control, which basically made Phillip, Whizzy and me Aevion's parents now.

"I'm sorry, Rachel. The princess has requested to see you," he spoke while staring at the floor and rubbing his tiny paws together nervously.

"This couldn't wait until I was dressed?" I quickly reached back, unlocked the door and pushed him outside with my hand. He covered his eyes as I slid him across the tile floor and onto the carpeted hallway. "Give me five minutes," I barked and then slammed the door.

I could hear him whimper and then scurry down the hallway towards my bedroom where Princess Merran was hiding.

Standing back in front of the mirror, I wiped away the condensation from the glass. My wet hair clung to my face, and my eyes were still red. There was a knock at the door.

"I said five minutes!" I snapped thinking Aevion had returned.

"Oh, I'm sorry, Rachel," Phillip's muffled voice replied through the door. "But I really need to go to the bathroom."

My heart started to flutter when I heard his voice. It was very strange. Only a year ago I wouldn't have cared if Phillip were here, but now things were different. He made me feel weird and I sort of liked it.

I took a deep breath, "Can't you go downstairs?"

He didn't respond immediately. "Ah...well. I'm not quite comfortable with that, Rachel," He replied. "I had to borrow Whizzy's clothes and they're...well, a little small."

I watched in the mirror as a smile crept across my face. I couldn't help it. I had to see this. Phillip was over six feet tall and Whizzy was shorter than me. Reaching out for the door handle I could feel myself begin to giggle. I stopped to gather myself and then grabbed hold of my towel across my chest and cracked the door open slightly to peer out. Catching a glimpse of Phillip standing there with an orange t-shirt that looked more like a tube top, I burst into laughter. His belly button was staring at me like a creepy eyeball. He also wore Christmas-themed pajama pants with Rudolph and Santa faces all over them. These were also too short and barely covered his knobby knees. He stood with his hands and arms covering his body as if he were naked. It was the strangest and funniest thing I had ever seen. It was kind of cute.

"Oh my gosh, Phillip. What did my brother do to you?" I was laughing pretty hard now and his face began to turn bright red. "Phillip...you look ridiculous."

"Can I go...please?" He begged as he danced on the carpet in his bare feet. "I'd go downstairs, but I can't let everyone see me like this."

"I'll hurry; just wait right there." I rushed back into the bathroom, finished drying off and hurriedly pulled on my night clothes...just an old t-shirt and sweatpants since I had long out grown the little girl night gowns. I didn't even dry my hair, but pulled it back in a ponytail.

Phillip was still hopping around like a frog in the hallway when I opened the door. His dance was quite silly, and it added to how goofy he looked in my brother's clothes. I so wished I had my phone to get video. The door slammed behind me, almost hitting my rear when I heard Phillip yell, "Thanks!"

In my bedroom, Princess Merran waited impatiently for my return. It was just like my mom would have done. Merran, a white cat, was curled up on my pillow with Aevion at the foot of the bed. She gracefully rose when I entered. The banished ex-queen was anxiously awaiting our return to Mistasia.

"Sorry I took so long...I was delayed, Princess," I started to bow then felt silly, so I stopped and then stumbled. It was really awkward which I am definitely glad Phillip didn't see...or my brother. Whizzy would have definitely made some joke about it. "What is it that you wanted to talk to me about?"

"Why does your grandpa wait to take us back to Mistasia, Rachel?" She was very forceful in her tone.

I was shocked to hear her so rude. That was not something she had ever done to me before.

"We need to return immediately!" She continued before I could answer.

"I know, Princess Merran. I want to go back too, but he said he wanted to wait until the morning when my parents are gone," I replied.

243

The cat tilted her head in a peculiar way. I instantly knew that she didn't understand why that was important.

"I fear that your grandpa has lost his courage, Rachel Whizzenmog."

"No...no, Princess. We can't just leave with my parents here. They will realize that we are missing. With my grandpa here, things are different. When it's just Whizzy and me, we have the freedom to...go play. So our parents expect us to be missing for some time. It is normal. They believe that we are just playing with friends. If my grandpa is missing, that would worry them." I wasn't sure if that even made sense to me so I was pretty sure that Princess Merran would probably be confused.

"It's like the difference between Grace and your servants at Cadieux Castle."

Her ears perked up.

"When Grace isn't at the castle you believe her to be off protecting it. When your servants are gone, you notice that there isn't someone taking care of your needs."

"Ah...I think I understand." She paused for a moment. "Does that mean your grandpa is your parents' servant?"

"No! No, I mean that he is someone that is expected to be around the castle and easily found when needed." I responded.

"Oh...I see."

"Princess, please. You must understand my grandpa will take us to Mistasia. I promise you that. He hasn't lost his courage," I added.

GREEN STONE

3

Later that night, I stood outside the door to the room where my grandpa slept. Whizzy and I had always known him as Grandpa, but he was the original Michael Whizzenmog. His middle name was Rainer. My dad is Michael Whizzenmog, junior, and my brother is the third.

There was a pounding in my chest as I stood, hesitantly, outside the door. I could feel my heart pumping blood through my body like a speeding roller coaster. It was something I had never noticed before our trips to Mistasia. Now everything seemed clearer...more noticeable. My senses were so focused. I wished I could be this focused in math class...maybe I wouldn't have gotten a "C" on my first semester exam.

It was 10:15 pm. Grandpa Whizzenmog was surely asleep, but I needed to know that he was still going. Something in my gut told me something was wrong. I could hear the sound of music from Whizzy's video game in the distance. I scanned the hallway before knocking. No one was around.

My body moved in slow motion. I softly tapped my knuckles on the door as if it was made of glass and afraid it would shatter.

"Why am I so nervous?" I muttered to myself. My hands felt sweaty. "This is ridiculous."

I felt like a criminal. All I wanted to do was talk with my grandpa about a secret magical world where an evil king has taken over and we are trying to overthrow him.

"Oh that's why I'm nervous...I sound crazy!" I answered my own question, which now I realize doesn't make me seem very sane in the first place.

The door opened.

I gasped.

"Rachel?" my grandpa questioned, sounding as surprised as I was to find me standing outside his door this late at night.

"Grandpa," I replied.

"Are you all right?"

I nodded, "Sorry to bother you. I'll go back to bed."

"My dear, come in." He placed his large hand on my shoulder. It seemed so light and delicate for something that resembled a bear claw in size.

He walked me to a single wooden chair at the desk along the wall. Then he sat on the bed. We remained quiet for a moment. I avoided his eyes, but I knew he was looking right at me. Instead I stared at a picture of our family sitting on the nightstand. It was my grandpa's. He had

brought it with him on his trip. That is
when I noticed this room looked like my
grandpa had lived in it for years. The covers
on the bed and curtains on the wall were
the same, a dark orange like the leaves in
fall. Yet, on the nightstand were his reading
glasses and chrome-colored watch. His
jacket was wrapped around the chair I sat
in. I could smell his aftershave on its collar.
He had made this room his home. That was
when I saw a strange object sitting next to
his glasses that I had never seen before. It
was small and dark green, yet it glowed like
a flame inside lighted it.

"Grandpa, what is that?"

"Ah...that is an emerald. It is a very
rare gemstone."

"Did it belong to Grandmother?" I
questioned. I couldn't remember her ever
talking about it, but she had died nearly five
years ago. Maybe I had just forgotten.

My grandpa changed the subject. "Rachel, what brings you to my door at this hour?" He raised his eyebrow.

I still couldn't look in his eyes. This whole situation was making me very uncomfortable. Was I really about to ask my grandpa, a man I loved and admired, if he was a coward? I must be insane to even believe Princess Merran for a second.

The emerald glimmered in the corner of my eye. Suddenly, I couldn't stop thinking about it. It was mesmerizing.

"Rachel!" My grandpa sternly called. "You are acting strangely...like your brother."

I laughed. I was acting very strangely, but lately everything in my life was strange. "Grandpa, why didn't you return to Mistasia?"

"Love," he answered without hesitation. "My priorities changed. I met your grandmother, had a family and moved far away from that life." He didn't appear to have any regrets, but tears formed in his aged eyes.

I didn't know if he was thinking about Grandma or Mistasia.

"Didn't you ever wonder what had happened in Mistasia?" I wanted to know how he left it behind so easily. I had been a wreck since we left and it had only been a few hours!

"I always knew it would find me."

"Find you?" I asked. "Why were you hiding?"

"Mistasia had changed. Everything had changed, my dear." He rubbed the back of his neck.

"How had Mistasia changed? What made you leave?" I needed to know. Mistasia was dangerous now, but only because my grandpa had left it unprotected.

"Sometimes one choice is all it takes to alter the course of everything, Rachel.

Just one." Then he stopped explaining. He seemed very upset.

We sat together silently for a few moments as my grandpa struggled to regain his composure. He rubbed his hand over his mouth and took a deep breath.

Finally, I spoke out, "It is time to return, Grandpa."

He nodded. "Off to bed now. We have quite a journey ahead of us tomorrow."

LEAVING GREENVILLE

4

My alarm began blaring at 7 am that following morning. I am sure that I don't have to explain how early that is when there is no school. Yet, my excitement drove me like it was Christmas morning. I leapt out of bed and dashed to my closet. Quickly changing out of my pajamas, I got dressed, grabbed my wand and went to leave my bedroom when I nearly tripped over Princess Merran. She stood at the door like she was waiting for me to open it. When I did, she gracefully exited. I rolled my eyes at her antics and headed for Whizzy's room.

Grandpa Whizzenmog met me in the hallway outside my brother's room. He, too, was dressed and ready for our trip.

"Do we dare enter?" He said with a smile.

"We had better knock," I replied back with a slight giggle.

He knocked on Whizzy's bedroom door three times. There was no reply.

"Whizzy! Phillip! It is time to go," I called so they would hear me through the door.

My grandpa reached for the door handle.

"Stop!" I blurted out. "Please, don't do that. What if he isn't...decent?"

"Whizzy? My dear he's been indecent since the day he was born." Then he rubbed my back to calm my nerves. "Just wait right here."

Then Grandpa Whizzenmog opened the door, stepped inside, gave me a sly wink and closed the door behind him. Next, his booming voice erupted from the bedroom. "Michael Whizzenmog, wake up!"

I could hear shouting, followed by crashing, and I think someone farted. The commotion continued for a few minutes. Then my grandpa came into the hallway and quickly slammed the door. He was covering his nose and mouth with his shirt. The door handle violently wiggled; then Phillip and Whizzy pounded on the door. They were trying to get out like some hideous creature was attempting to eat them alive.

"What is wrong? What happened?" I screamed in a panic.

"Open this door, Grandpa!" Whizzy yelled in a fit of rage.

"You must pay the penalty for keeping us from our departing time, Michael Whizzenmog." Grandpa chuckled heartily with his nose and mouth still covered within his shirt. His eyes were watering when he looked at me.

I gave him a shocked expression and shook my head.

"It was Whizzy's alarm...do I have to pay the penalty, sir?" Phillip cried.

"Sorry, my boy. Guilt by association." He cackled like a high school freshman.

"What did you do?" I scolded.

"Just gave the boy some of his own medicine."

"Did you fart?" I was most disgusted to imagine my grandpa intentionally passing gas and then trapping my brother and Phillip inside the room to suffer. "Open the door!"

His laughter was growing with every second.

"Now!" I shouted like my mom.

The door flung open causing Phillip and Whizzy to crash to the floor gasping for air. Phillip crawled down the hallway.

"What did you eat?" Phillip squealed in a girlish voice.

"That...was...awful," Whizzy said between deep breaths of fresh air. "I'm gonna get you back, Grandpa."

"Son, you can't beat the master," my grandpa replied, patting Whizzy on top of the head.

"I hope that isn't your power in Mistasia," Whizzy blurted out. "Well, actually that would be pretty cool." He pointed at our giggling elder. "Just don't use it on us...remember, we are on your side."

"You two are embarrassing," I yelled. "Let's just go, please. We have to get to Mistasia and you guys are screwing around."

It was December 16th and my parents had gone to finish their holiday shopping. They would be gone all day. It made today our best opportunity to travel to Mistasia and hopefully return before my parents could realize that we had disappeared.

"We have around ten hours in Greenville," I explained.

"Good that gives us about ten days in Mistasia then," Whizzy replied. "That isn't too bad."

We had gathered in the basement...that was, everyone except Grandpa Whizzenmog.

"Where is your grandpa, Rachel?" Princess Merran questioned.

As we looked around, he finally appeared at the top of the stairs. We watched as he slowly maneuvered the staircase and walked across the basement to the sliding glass door that had served as the portal to Mistasia for our previous trips.

I watched as he adjusted his gloves and then grabbed the handle to the door.

"What are you doing?" I asked.

"I am opening the door," he said with a smart tone.

Whizzy and I shared a confused glance.

"But we have to go through the door," Whizzy said before I could.

"That is the portal to Mistasia, Rainer Whizzenmog," Princess Merran added.

"Well, we can't really go back through the same way you came out can we? Weren't you all banished?" He slid the door open and walked out into the cold winter air.

Phillip was the first to follow. Then we all proceeded to walk out into our wintry backyard.

I carried Princess Merran in my arms, and Aevion sat on Phillip's shoulder. We didn't talk much. Instead we just followed my grandpa as he walked through the backyard and into the forest.

It was cold and slightly windy. It had apparently snowed last night, as a fresh layer of white fluffy snow hung on the tree branches above our heads. A pile of snow slid

off one tree and landed directly in front of
Phillip.

"That was close," Phillip said,
sounding relieved it didn't land on his head.
Then more snow tumbled from the same
tree and hit Whizzy. Phillip and I laughed at
Whizzy as he brushed the snow from his
hair.

"That's not funny!" my brother yelled.
He looked up into the trees. They swayed in
the wind. More snow began to fall toward
us. Phillip, Whizzy and I dashed away just in
time.

"Where are we going, Whizzy?" Phillip
spoke out the side of his mouth. He looked
worried. "Your grandpa isn't gonna smoke
us out again, is he?"

How disgusting...boys and their bodily
functions. How could someone be so proud
when they make a room smell so badly that
no one can even breathe?

"I know; it was like rotten cabbage and dead animals!" Whizzy laughed.

"Don't say dead animals," Phillip gulped. "We're all gonna be animals when we get back to Mistasia, and I don't wanna be dead!" He cried.

We were silent again. I knew we all were thinking about what Phillip had just said. Everyone looked worried.

"I don't think we can just walk to Mistasia," Whizzy snarled in an attempt to be funny and lighten the mood.

It didn't work.

"No, we cannot, Whizzy. It is just up ahead," Grandpa Whizzenmog responded.

"The river?" I muttered. "But it is frozen over."

"Water makes for a strong magical conductor, Rachel," Grandpa Whizzenmog explained.

"Condu-what?" Whizzy showed how little he paid attention in science class.

"A conductor, Whizzy. It is something that allows another force...in this case magic, to flow properly. Even with the water being frozen, it will let the magic in my wand through...sometimes even magnifying its power," Our grandpa elaborated as he stepped up to the river's edge.

"I'm not really liking this whole jumping into a frozen river idea," Whizzy whined.

"Then you don't have to come," Grandpa Whizzenmog replied. "You can stay home and help your parents wrap gifts." He turned back and smiled at me. I loved it when he picked on Whizzy.

Grandpa Whizzenmog adjusted his snowcap and then pulled a straight wooden stick from his boot. It was his wand. He studied it longingly. It must have been decades since he used it. Running his fingers

along the length of his wand, he inhaled
deeply.

"Let's see if I remember how to use
this," he said.

FLUSHED AWAY

5

I stood impatiently behind my grandpa as he looked out across the frozen river. Drifts of snow swelled on the far side of the river, but there was very little at our feet. Phillip and Whizzy were standing on either side of me as the wind blew at our backs, sweeping the snow across the ice. It slithered along the frozen river top like a snake in the sand. The sun was very low and dim in the sky.

I squinted to see what Grandpa Whizzenmog was doing as he reached into his pocket for something. When he found it, he quickly moved onto the ice.

"What is he waiting for?" Whizzy crassly remarked.

I didn't have any idea. No one did, because none of us responded.

Phillip, Whizzy and I stayed back on shore.

"Do not follow me, kids. I will make sure it is safe first." He stopped only a few feet away from us when a strong gust of wind swirled around and engulfed him in snow.

"Grandpa!" Whizzy yelled then started to run on the ice.

I grabbed him by the arm, "Wait! Don't move!"

The snow blew into the air and Grandpa Whizzenmog reappeared. He had huddled and covered his face.

"I'm fine. Please, stay there," He commanded while wiping snow from his eyes and beard.

The winds had caught us by surprise. Phillip was cuddling Aevion to his chest and I knelt down and huddled around Princess

Merran. Snow was flying around like we were in a winter tornado. It was somewhat difficult to see until my grandpa pulled something from his pocket.

A bright green light made the fluffy white snow seem to disappear. It shot rays of dark green light into the river.

"What is that?" Phillip croaked. He seemed very nervous. I didn't like it when he was nervous...I liked him better when he was confident.

My grandpa raised his arm into the air. He was chanting something, although I couldn't hear him, I could see his lips moving. The light from the object in his hands grew brighter and brighter just before he slammed it onto the frozen river with a loud grunt. A circle of green light rippled out from the object, shaking the ground like a tremor when it passed us by.

"That was wicked!" Whizzy shouted.

Grandpa stood up and backed away with his wand still in his left hand. He eagerly studied the small green object now sticking out from the ice.

"It's the emerald!" I shouted above the rushing winds.

"What?" Phillip asked.

Whizzy and Phillip each listened intently, "A green emerald. I saw it in Grandpa's room last night," I explained as my hair whipped against the increasing winds. "I asked if it belonged to Grandmother, but he didn't say."

Small cracks began to splinter in the ice. They stretched out from the center where the emerald had pierced the ice. The river began to change colors like it was melting rapidly. A large circle formed near where my grandpa now stood.

"Hurry!" Grandpa Whizzenmog shouted as he emphatically waved us toward him.

We dashed onto the icy river and slid to a stop next to the only person who seemed to have any idea what was happening beneath us.

I saw the water bubbling and swirling under our feet. It changed colors directly below us, from a white to clear like the sliding glass door in our basement.

"Hold on!" I heard my grandpa's voice shout, as he firmly grabbed a hold of my arm.

A sinking feeling came over me. Now I knew how Phillip felt almost every single day in school. My stomach flipped and I suddenly felt sick when I watched the icy river-top disintegrate under my boots.

I screamed as I fell into the river, which now swirled like a whirlpool. The water was all around me, yet I wasn't wet or cold. We were in a portal. Grandpa had done it...he had opened the portal to Mistasia.

An orange fish flew past my face. I screamed and then covered my mouth for fear of drowning, but I could breath.

I watched as Whizzy flipped around doing somersaults. He smiled so widely that I almost didn't recognize him. Phillip, however, looked terrified.

Colors began to fade. My brother and Phillip grew smaller until I could no longer see them. Then everything went dark.

Thud!

FIND OUT MORE ABOUT
THE LAND OF MISTASIA
@
www.LandOfMistasia.com

PHILLIP & WHIZZY TRILOGY

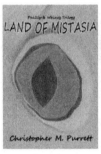  

PHILLIP & WHIZZY SHORT STORIES

 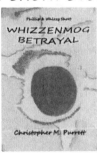

ABOUT THE AUTHOR

CHRISTOPHER M. PURRETT

Christopher attended college at Central Michigan University, graduating with a degree in Broadcast & Cinematic Arts. There he met his wife,

Misty, with whom he had two daughters, Lea & Kyra. The Phillip & Whizzy characters were born when he began telling bedtime stories to his daughters.

In his spare time, Christopher loves music, movies and sports, especially hockey and football. He lives in Michigan with his family.

Keep up with him at www.ChristopherMPurrett.com
Twitter
www.Twitter.com/CMPurrett
Facebook
www.Facebook.com/ChristopherMPurrett

50916434R00152

Made in the USA
Lexington, KY
05 April 2016